EMMANUEL MCCLUE
and
The Mystery of the Shroud

By
Tony McCaffrey

Ambassador Books, Inc.
Worcester • Massachusetts

ISBN 1-929039-08-5

Library of Congress Cataloging-in-Publication Data

McCaffrey, Tony.
  Emmanuel McClue and the mystery of the Shroud / by Tony McCaffrey.
      p. cm.
Summary: Twelve-year-old Emmanuel McClue's parents are participating in an investigation of miracles that thrusts him into a world of excitement and danger.
  ISBN 1-929039-08-5
  [1. Holy Shroud--Fiction. 2. Cloning--Fiction. 3. Racially mixed people--Fiction. 4. Mystery and detective stories.] I. Title.
  PZ7.M122837 Em 2001
  [Fic]--dc21
                                   2001005352

Cover illustrated by Alan Colavecchio
Published in 2001 in the United States by Ambassador Books, Inc.
71 Elm Street, Worcester, Massachusetts 01609
(800) 577-0909
Printed in Canada.

For current information about all titles from Ambassador Books, Inc. visit our website at: www.ambassadorbooks.com.

Dedication

To the Jesuits, who guided me into the adventure of God.

A Brush with Evil

FROM THE SMALL CONTROL ROOM, DR. MARSHALL McClue and Dr. Graciela Cruz-McClue looked through the one-way glass onto a strange sight. In the next room, two priests leaned over a nineteen-year-old boy, who was strapped down to a bed. The priests took turns reciting prayers from the books they were holding. The boy lay quietly staring off toward a point on the ceiling.

"How are the sound levels?" Roger Thigpen asked. He was also in the control room, and he guided the McClues on operating the equipment.

"Good," Graciela said. "I can hear the prayers clearly."

"Let's test the remote cameras," Roger said. "He's going to act up any minute now. Camera one. Panning?"

"Check," Marshall said.

"Zooming?" Roger asked.

"Check," Marshall said. "In and out."

As they tested the other two cameras, Graciela looked around. The room resembled a simple master control room of a TV studio. Graciela sat before a soundboard with many control levers and bouncing needles. She had not been in a TV studio control room since her high school days in El Salvador where she sometimes sang for a local TV station. This was no TV studio. It was built to record an exorcism, the process of removing a demon from a person. The room was not much wider than a closet. Graciela could stretch out her arms and touch both walls. It wasn't too cramped for her, though. She was 5 feet 5 inches tall and petite. Her husband, however, was bumping his knees against the bottom of the table as he sat in front of the controls for the three remote-controlled cameras. His six-foot-three African-American frame made him look like an eighth grader sitting at a third grader's desk.

Graciela looked through the one-way glass into the larger room on the other side. A heavily padded bed was the only furniture in the room. The floor was plain wood. The windows were narrow slits four inches wide, much too narrow to squeeze through. Still, the windows had bars over them. Every precaution had been taken. The remote-controlled cameras had been fixed to the ceiling because it was too dangerous to put real camera operators in the room.

"You're from Boston I understand," Roger said. "Welcome to London. I hope what you're about to see won't be your only impression of London."

Roger checked the tape machine to see if the cameras and microphones were actually recording.

"What are your backgrounds?" Roger asked.

"I'm a medical doctor," Graciela said. "Marshall has a Ph.D. in chemistry and most recently worked at the Boston Crime Lab."

"Well, I hope you don't mind me saying so but even your training will be no preparation for what you will see today," Roger said as he bent over to check the cable connections.

Roger straightened up and looked through the one-way glass at the trance-like boy lying on the bed. "Who do you work for?" he asked.

Graciela and Marshall looked awkwardly at each other.

"The funder of our investigations wants to remain anonymous," Marshall replied.

"Whoever it is must be pretty influential," Roger said. "Not just anyone is allowed to come into this room."

"Not just anyone can *fit* into this room," Marshall said.

Roger glanced at Marshall and laughed.

"Sorry about that," Roger said.

Suddenly, the boy on the bed strained against the straps, picked up his head and looked at one of the priests.

"Here we go," Roger said. "Camera two, medium shot."

"Roger, Roger," Marshall chuckled. "Sorry, I couldn't help it." Their jokes relieved the nervousness in the room.

"It's all right," Roger said. "I get that a lot."

The boy seemed to stare right through Father Barry Owens. His eyes glared and his jaw was set with tension. He spoke intensely, like a baseball manager yelling in an umpire's face. Father Barry continued to pray without seeming to notice.

"I can't understand what he's saying," Graciela said.

"Boost the levels on the mikes," Roger said.

A low, intense, warbling voice could be heard in the control room. Still no words could be understood.

"I'll boost the levels to the maximum," Graciela said.

The dark voice became louder but still not understandable. The boy seemed to spit hate and venom in Father Barry's direction.

"I don't see how Father Barry can just stand there," Graciela said. "I'm getting chills just listening from the safety of this room."

"The demon will do anything to distract the priests," Roger said. "Anything to make them falter or doubt. Right now, it's its only defense."

"Too bad we can't understand what he's saying," Marshall said.

"We've got it on tape," Roger said. "We'll give it to our language experts. It could be a foreign language or an ancient language. For all I know, it could even be English, only spoken backwards."

"Marshall, get a close-up of Dennis's face on camera one," Roger said.

Marshall looked quizzically at Roger.

"That's his name, Dennis, but that's not his face. Well, it is but it isn't." Roger said.

"What do you mean?" Graciela asked.

"Six months ago, Dennis was basically a normal nineteen-year-old, a little rebellious, a few brushes with the law, but nothing serious. Anyway, we have home movies. That voice is not quite Dennis's voice. We've compared the tapes and digitally analyzed the two wave-forms. And that face, it's just not quite the same. The expressions, the muscle tone, and the eyes—oh, the eyes. Digitally overlaying the two images brings out the differences." Roger said.

The boy turned his head away from Father Barry and toward the priest on the other side, Father Dennis. Mitchell, as if noticing him for the first time.

"Nice name, Padre," taunted the demon in Dennis, this time speaking in perfectly understandable English. "We've got a lot in common. They say I'm a menace. Well, you're a menace, too."

Father Dennis Mitchell ignored him and continued reciting prayers in sync with Father Barry.

"Father, bother, Dennis, menace," chanted the demon in ever louder tones trying to drown out the priests' words. Some of the demon's words were much worse than that. "Father, bother, Dennis, menace. FATHER, BOTHER, DENNIS, MENACE."

"What's happened to him?" Marshall asked.

"He started hearing voices and seeing things," Roger said. "Then, he had wild mood swings, went into fits of rage, hit people, broke things, and claimed to have no memory of what happened. After several medical exams and three or four psychiatrists, it became clear that medical science could not help him."

"FATHER DENNIS THE BOTHERING MEN-ACE!"the demon screamed over and over again.

Roger hesitated a moment before he continued, "We got special permission to record the exorcism to see what we can learn about doing exorcisms more effectively. That boy in there has been going through six months of total chaos and darkness."

Suddenly, the demon was quiet. The boy lay on his back breathing heavily, trying to catch his breath. The priests continued to pray, speaking more forcefully, as if sensing some progress. The three in the control room were relieved by the silence.

Abruptly, the demon raised his head again and looked directly at the one-way glass as if he could see into the control room.

"Don't worry," Roger said, "he can't see us in here."

"Dr. Marshall McClue, I presume," the demon said smugly. "I hope you're getting some good pictures. Is my best side showing?"

Marshall felt the hair on the back of his neck stand up.

"I didn't *think* he could see us," Roger corrected.

"And your lovely wife, Dr. Graciela," continued the demon in a falsely pleasant voice.

Graciela felt her skin crawl as she began to stand up.

"Steady," Roger said. "It's only an attempt to distract us."

"A pair of doctors in the family," continued the sugary tone. "How nice."

"Concentrate," Roger coached. "Focus on your controls."

"And how's your son Emmanuel?" the demon asked in a sickly sweet voice.

A dark presence filled the control room. A pressure weighed down on Graciela, and the small room seemed to become unbearably smaller. Her head swam. A moment before she was a detached observer. Now, the safe boundaries had disappeared. The demon knew her name. It knew her son's name. What else did it know? What else could it do? She felt violated by the demon's knowledge. She tried to remain calm and professional.

"Left him downstairs?" the demon's voice turned deep and nasty. "Think he's safe? Think again!"

Graciela bolted from her chair and frantically opened the door at the back of the room. Marshall was up and two steps behind her. As they raced from the room, they heard the demon's loud howl and cackle. The demon was truly enjoying what it was doing.

Graciela ran down one large marble stairway after another. Marshall was in quick pursuit. Even though Marshall's legs were much longer than Graciela's, he could not catch her.

"Emmanuel," she called out as she rounded the landing of one set of stairs and started down another. After three flights of stairs, they reached the first floor and sprinted down the hallway. The faces of priests seemed to stare at them from the row of oil paintings that lined the dark wood walls.

They came to the room where Emmanuel was studying. The door was closed. Graciela turned the doorknob, but the door would not open. Marshall tried with the same result. Then, Marshall put his shoulder to the door and it unstuck, swinging open. A notebook and pre-algebra book were neatly laid out on a beautiful oak table. Pencils, pens, erasers, but no Emmanuel. An empty chair was pushed back away from the table.

Marshall looked behind the door then under the table.

"Emmanuel," Graciela shouted as they scurried out of the room to continue the search.

It was a long hallway with closed doors on each side. Graciela took the right side while Marshall took the left side. They raced from one room to the next, opening doors and calling out, "Emmanuel."

Room after room, door slam after door slam, their search continued to the end of the hallway. No success. At the end of the hallway were the large double doors to the small chapel. They hurried inside. Their eyes took a while to adjust to the low light in the chapel. Although it was called the small chapel, it was bigger than some parish churches. It could seat three hundred. Graciela moved briskly up the main aisle passing pew after pew. Her head darted back and forth searching frantically. Marshall hurried after her.

"Emmanuel," she called out. The sound echoed off the marble in the massive space.

"Emmanuel," he called out. The two voices raced after each other.

As if on cue, a small head popped up from the second pew. There he was. Emmanuel. Behind him, there was a statue of Jesus with outstretched arms. To Graciela, it looked as if Jesus was watching over her son. She ran to him and took him in her arms. She held him close and rocked him. Emmanuel, who was just a few days shy of his twelfth birthday, did not remember being held this tightly since he was a small child.

"There you are, my Emmanuel," Graciela said in a relieved voice. "*Gracias a Dios.*"

"I needed a break from fractions," Emmanuel said, starting to defend himself.

"You're not in trouble," Marshall reassured him, as he stood over Emmanuel and Graciela. He placed his big, strong hands gently on their shoulders. "We're just very glad to see you."

Graciela finally released Emmanuel from her smothering hug. The three walked out of the chapel side by side. Graciela had her arm around Emmanuel's shoulders, keeping him close to her side. Emmanuel was suspicious of what had happened because of his mom's extreme reaction, but now did not seem the time to ask. So, he just offered his side of the story as they strolled down the aisle.

"I was bored with fractions," began Emmanuel. "I snooped around and found this cool chapel. When I lay down, I saw that the ceiling was filled with angels. I imagined what it would be like to fly. I must have fallen asleep. Next thing I knew, you came flying in."

Graciela and Marshall smiled at their son's banter.

Later that evening in their hotel room, Marshall and Graciela quietly discussed the events of the day. They sat across from each other at a small table near the window. The only light in the room was a lamp hanging over the table that separated them. Two beds filled out the hotel room.

In the bed farthest from his parents, Emmanuel lay on his back with his eyes closed and the covers pulled up to his chin. He pretended to be asleep. He got some of his best information this way, playing the sleeping spy.

"I don't care if we lose our funding," Graciela said. "We're quitting this case."

"I absolutely agree," Marshall said. "I just want us to be very clear that we may lose everything."

"We both agreed that Emmanuel's safety comes first," Graciela said. "And that *thing* threatened him today."

Emmanuel couldn't help but jerk a little when he heard that statement. But he recovered by turning it into a smooth rollover from his back to his side so he faced them. Graciela and Marshall stopped talking and looked at Emmanuel. When it was clear he was still asleep, or so they thought, they continued their conversation in hushed tones.

"I couldn't agree more," Marshall said.

"This is not what I had in mind when I quit my job at Massachusetts General Hospital," Graciela said.

"I'll contact our benefactor's lawyer first thing tomorrow," said Marshall.

"We are supposed to investigate miracles," Graciela said. "This is the furthest thing from a miracle."

"If the exorcism is successful that might be considered miraculous," Marshall said.

"I want to investigate goodness and signs of God's presence," Graciela said. "I already know there's evil in the world."

"The two are related," Marshall said.

"But the nerve of our benefactor," Graciela said. "On our very first case to assign us pure evil."

"Hopefully, we'll be able to choose our next case," Marshall said. "It says in our contract that being assigned would be rare."

Graciela abruptly switched subjects. "We've got to get a tutor for Emmanuel," she said. "He can't just sit around doing schoolwork by himself all day long."

"Don't we have some prospects here in London?" Marshall asked.

"Yes, I've lined up a couple of interviews for tomorrow morning, then we're back home to Boston," Graciela said. She looked at her son. "He looks so peaceful."

Emmanuel did his best to remain still and look like a sweet angel.

"I hope we're doing the right thing," Graciela said. "We've uprooted him from his school and all his friends, and for what, to search the world for miracles."

"We've been through this before. There are not many eleven-year-olds who get to travel the world on exciting adventures," Marshall said.

"After today, I know there are certain kinds of adventures I don't want him experiencing," his wife said.

"We've made special arrangements for him to stay in touch with his friends, and we come back home between assignments," Marshall reassured.

"I know, I know," Graciela said. "But still I wonder...."

The E-Zone

By the time Emmanuel woke up, Marshall was already out of the room. Graciela was dressed for the day and was sitting at the small table looking through her organizer. Emmanuel did not make a very good spy in the morning. His parents had been moving around him showering and dressing, and Emmanuel detected nothing. His spy work would have to be done at a different time.

"Where's Dad?" Emmanuel asked as he rubbed his eyes and tried to sit up.

"He's down in the restaurant having breakfast and reading the paper," Graciela said. "I had my breakfast first while your father stayed here with you. I brought up some juice and bagels for you."

"How long have you been up?" Emmanuel asked, sensing that much had happened while he slept.

"About two hours," Graciela said.

"Two hours," groaned Emmanuel who stopped trying to sit up and let himself fall back onto the bed.

"Here comes the list of what they've done," Emmanuel thought.

Graciela got up and began to pack the three suitcases that were lined up on her neatly made bed.

"Well," Graciela said, "I called the two possible tutors for you and arranged interviews in the hotel restaurant."

She looked at her watch.

"The first one will be here in twenty-five minutes," Graciela said. "Let's see some movement over there."

Emmanuel rolled over, hunkered down, and pulled the blanket over him as a shield against the morning world.

"I called the airlines and bought tickets for our flight back to Boston later today," Graciela said.

"I thought we were here for another week," came Emmanuel's muffled voice from beneath the blankets.

"We've done all we can on this case," Graciela said. "This way we'll be back in Boston for your birthday. Won't that be nice?"

"Nice move, Mom," Emmanuel thought. *"Smoothly changing the topic to my birthday to distract me from why we're leaving this case after one day. I'll let you get away with it for now."*

Of course, Graciela did not tell Emmanuel about Marshall's call to Roger Thigpen. Marshall called Roger and informed him of their decision to quit the case and apologized to him for any inconvenience it would cause his work. Roger understood and apologized to Marshall, for no one knew beforehand that the demon could see, or at least, sense people behind the one-way glass. Nor did Graciela tell Emmanuel how Marshall e-mailed their benefactor's lawyer, Ms. Madeline Downey and informed her of their decision.

Emmanuel's parents were extremely efficient and professional. In one night, they talked over and basically replanned their whole life. They were open to the possibility of losing their job and were ready to face it. They moved so quickly in their plans that it often made Emmanuel tired just trying to keep up with them. He felt he needed to watch a daily 'McClue Family Newscast' so he could stay current.

Graciela came over to the lump beneath the blankets.

"Here comes the poke-tickle-slap," Emmanuel thought. Sure enough, Graciela first poked him in the back with her finger. Next, she tickled him in the ribs with both hands. Finally, she slapped him lightly on the butt as she walked away. It was a ritual of hers. Emmanuel knew that it was her final, friendly wake-up call before she would start to lose her temper. It was a two-minute warning and, Emmanuel knew he better get vertical and move toward the shower very soon. Emmanuel wished that his parents gave such clear signals all the time.

He managed to will himself to the standing position. It wasn't so bad once he got himself moving and his body took over on automatic pilot. He stumbled into the bathroom and turned on the shower. He took a two-minute shower, whether he needed it or not. Once he tried to just run the water for two minutes without getting in. But his mom did not fall for that. So, he did what it took to get by her. He washed his face and neck, added a few swipes of the soap on his arms and chest, and shampooed his hair.

He emerged from the bathroom with a towel wrapped around him and found his clothes for the day laid out on his bed. Taking them back in the bathroom, he dressed then came out to fill his pockets with his stuff: comb, handkerchief, a couple of bite-size chocolate bars, and a small rubber ball for when he was bored. It was a simple toy, but he never got tired of bouncing it.

Emmanuel went over to the small table, took a sip of orange juice, and spread cream cheese on his bagel. Graciela was busy moving about the room packing. Emmanuel took his bagel and went out onto the balcony to look at the view. They were on the third floor of the hotel overlooking the parking lot. A slight wind was blowing and the fresh air felt good on Emmanuel's face. A pigeon flew gracefully by gliding against the wind. What a thing to be able to fly! Emmanuel pondered the physics of flight for a moment, then felt the dry bagel in his mouth and went back inside for more orange juice.

On the small table next to his glass were several pieces of paper. Emmanuel glanced at the hotel brochure, but another paper caught his eye. In large type centered at the top of a cream-colored sheet was the name "Wilfred Charles Rigby." Beneath his name, also centered, was an address and phone number.

"*This must be one of the tutors,*" Emmanuel thought, "*and this must be what Mom calls a resume.*" The rest of the sheet was filled with dates, names of schools, and city names.

"Middle names are funny," Emmanuel thought. *"Why do we need them? Two names are enough. Three names together seem too big for just one person. Are the two names pregnant? There seems to be one and a half people there. Emmanuel Javier McClue. Javier? Who needs Javier? Who uses it? I don't feel like a Javier. If someone called that name in a crowd, I wouldn't respond. If I called Wilfred Charles Rigby by the name Charles, I bet he wouldn't respond."*

He looked up and spotted a pigeon that was perched on the railing of the balcony. Emmanuel froze. He wanted to get closer but feared that any movement would startle the bird. So, the two just stared at each other. The bird dipped and cocked its head this way and that, but never took its eye off Emmanuel.

Emmanuel slowly reached down and grabbed the hotel brochure. With slow and steady movements so as not to scare the bird, he folded a paper airplane out of the glossy paper. If he could not get any closer to the bird, he would sail a paper airplane near it to show the bird that he could fly, too. He finished folding the airplane and raised his hand to fling it.

"Emmanuel," Graciela said, her head buried in the suitcase. The bird fluttered away at the sound of her voice.

"Our first interview is in five minutes," she said. "Are you almost ready?"

"Yes," Emmanuel sighed.

He took the paper airplane out onto the balcony and heaved it. He threw it with the wind, so it took off quickly but soon it caught a down draft and dove straight into the parking lot pavement below. "*Ah, better to throw into the wind,*" Emmanuel thought. He returned to the small table eager to make another plane.

He took Mr. Rigby's resume and began to fold it into a plane. "*Mom's certainly read this,*" he thought.

A similar sheet was beneath Mr. Rigby's, but it was on white paper and had a different name centered across the top, "Jordana Marie Jamison." Another middle name. It must be the other tutor.

Emmanuel took the Rigby plane out onto the balcony and heaved it straight into the wind. Meeting the oncoming wind sent it angling high into the air. It continued angling until it looped like a roller coaster, flew upside down and headed back in the direction it started. It began to lose altitude quickly, making a forty-five degree angle to the ground where it crashed onto the hood of a blue car. It looked like a fighter plane crashing on the deck of an aircraft carrier. Emmanuel imagined sparks and flames, sirens and fire extinguishers. It skidded off the hood of the car and down onto the pavement in the neighboring empty parking space. Immediately, a pale green car pulled into the empty space and covered the paper plane.

A head of gray, slicked-back hair got out of the car. A tweed three-piece suit became visible as the driver stood up.

"*That Rigby plane was cool,*" Emmanuel thought. He was back at the table in an instant folding the resume of "Jordana Marie Jamison" into a plane. He returned to the balcony in a flash with the Jamison jet.

"Emmanuel, what are you doing?" Graciela asked. "Are you littering?"

What to Emmanuel was landing jet fighters on aircraft carriers was to his mom merely littering.

"You're going to pick up everything you threw off that balcony," Graciela scolded. "Emmanuel, what were you thinking?"

"This is the first fun I've had in days," Emmanuel thought.

"You'll have to pick up those things later," Graciela said. "We've got to get to the restaurant for the interview."

Graciela came over to the small table and looked down.

"Where are the resumes?" Graciela asked. "Give me that." She snatched the paper from his hand and unfolded it.

"We need this for the interview," Graciela said. "Emmanuel, how could you? Where's the other . . . ? Emmanuel Javier McClue!"

"That's it," Emmanuel thought, as he zoned out in his own thoughts while Mom continued her lecture. *"That's what middle names are for. Parents give their children middle names so when they are angry, they have enough words to get their anger out. It wouldn't be enough to say, 'Emmanuel.' It wouldn't be enough to say, 'Emmanuel McClue.' No, you have to say 'Emmanuel Javier McClue.' That's enough to carry the anger. Your parents will tell you that your middle name names you after your uncle or grandfather. Now you know the real reason. I think kids with short names get grounded more because the parents don't get their anger out, so they have to do more. If*

that's the case, give me more names. I'll take four, five, six, ten. Whatever it takes. Load me down with names. It's better than being grounded . . . . "

". . . your father. Emmanuel, are you listening to me?" Graciela scolded. "You're in the e-zone again, aren't you? You'd better be listening."

Emmanuel was very observant at times, but he was very spacey at times, too. His mom called his spacing out 'Emmanuel in the ozone,' or the Emmanuel zone, or the e-zone, for short. "Earth to Emmanuel. Earth to Emmanuel," she would often say when she was in a playful mood. She was not playing around now, though. A certain look on Emmanuel's face gave the e-zone away. His head was tilted slightly to the left. His eyes looked up and slightly to the right. Emmanuel always wrote down his e-zone thoughts then e-mailed them to his best friend, Chauncy Phillips, back in Boston. The middle name theory would be a good addition to his e-zone journal. Chauncy would enjoy this particular e-zone e-mail.

"Are you listening to me?" Graciela continued. "You're going down there to find Mr. Rigby's resume. We need it. Let's go. Now!"

She put Ms. Jamison's resume in her leather bound notebook to try to flatten it. They went out into the hall. Emmanuel took a couple of steps toward the elevator, but she corrected him.

"We're taking the stairs," Graciela said.

"*Good,*" Emmanuel thought. "*The stairs will help her get out her energy.*"

By the time they reached the last flight of stairs, his mom had calmed down a bit. The exercise had done some good.

"Do you have anything to say for yourself?" Graciela asked.

"I'm sorry, Mom," Emmanuel said. "I didn't know what a resume was, but I shouldn't throw anything from the balcony. I'm sorry."

With her body language she seemed to accept the apology, but she said nothing. She opened the door at the bottom of the stairs. It went out into the parking lot. She stood in the doorway with her arms crossed, while holding the door open with her body. Emmanuel ran outside and tried to locate the blue car next to the pale green one. After a moment, he did so and made a beeline in their direction. He could feel his mother watching his every move.

He looked on the ground all around the blue car. There was nothing there. He looked all around the pale green car. Nothing. He could feel an imaginary clock ticking away. It would not be much longer before his mom would call out to him. He lay on his stomach on the pavement and looked under the pale green car. There. He spotted the cream-colored airplane with its tip under the inside of the front tire. He tried to free it. No way. Not with a ton of steel on top of it. Finally, he ripped the tip off and pulled the paper out. The torn paper was now missing all the information at the top: Mr. Rigby's name, address, and phone. Not only that, but the pale green car was leaking oil, so several drops of dark oil had splattered on the paper.

"Emmanuel," Graciela called, whose inner ticking clock had gone off.

Emmanuel ran over and delivered the paper. She grimaced at it, then knelt down to wipe off the oil onto the grass. He dusted himself off and his mother joined in, dusting a little too forcefully in Emmanuel's opinion. Graciela flattened the paper and placed it in her leather-bound notebook on top of Ms. Jamison's resume.

Jordana the Joker

EMMANUEL AND GRACIELA PROCEEDED INTO THE hotel restaurant on the first floor. Marshall and another gentleman were sipping coffee across a table from each other. The gentleman had gray, slicked-back hair and wore a tweed suit. It was the driver of the pale green car. It was Mr. Rigby! Mr. Rigby had driven over his own resume!

"Mr. Rigby," Graciela said. "I am so sorry we're late. One of us had a little trouble getting up this morning."

Graciela looked Emmanuel's way and laughed. Mr. Rigby did not smile and showed no understanding that he knew the struggles of being a parent. Graciela sensed a dead end, so she tried another route.

"I'm Graciela McClue, and this is our son Emmanuel," she said as she reached out to shake his hand. Mr. Rigby stood up. He was very tall, 6 feet 4 inches and very slender.

"Charmed," Mr. Rigby said as he first shook Graciela's hand and then Emmanuel's. His hand felt stiff and cold.

"What shall we call you?" Graciela asked as she and Emmanuel took their seats at the table. Mr. Rigby sat back down.

"I go by W. Charles Rigby," Mr. Rigby said. "I'd be pleased if you call me Charles. The lad may call me Mr. Charles."

"*The middle name thing again*," Emmanuel thought. "*This man actually goes by his middle name.*"

Emmanuel sat next to Mr. Rigby. Marshall was already seated across from him, and Graciela sat next to Marshall. She placed the leather-bound notebook so the bottom was in her lap and the top leaned against the tabletop's edge. When she opened it, Mr. Rigby could not see his mangled resume. Marshall saw it, and his eyes opened wide with surprise although he said nothing.

"Mr. Rigby," Graciela said, "my husband and I will be teaching Emmanuel math and science. We are looking for someone to teach him literature, language arts, and history. Our research will take us around the world so we need someone who is extremely flexible with regard to travel. Your resume is quite impressive."

Graciela looked down at the stained and torn sheet of paper.

"I see you have extensive experience teaching at both the high school and university level," Graciela said. "Emmanuel will be turning twelve in a few days, so he is a bit younger than the students you normally teach."

She looked up from the resume. "What literature would you assign Emmanuel to read?" she asked.

"Shakespeare, of course," Mr. Rigby said, "Jane Austen, Charles Dickens, the Brontë sisters, Gerard Manley Hopkins."

"Would he read anything that is not British?" Marshall asked.

"Ah, quite," Mr. Rigby stammered, "Of course. I see. Indeed. I suppose we could throw in the Russians: Tolstoy, Dostoevsky."

"What would we do for fun?" Emmanuel asked, catching Mr. Rigby off-guard.

"We'd uh, we'd uh," Mr. Rigby hesitated, "go to book stores to read and drink tea."

"Are you able to travel?" Marshall asked.

"Yes," Mr. Rigby said, "my wife of thirty-six years passed away a year ago. I am not only able to travel; I would love to travel."

"I'm sorry to hear about your wife," Graciela said.

"Do you have any questions for us?" Marshall asked.

"I can assure you that by the time I am finished teaching your lad," Mr. Rigby said, "he will be versed in all the classics."

"Okay then," Marshall said, "I think that covers everything. We'll call you when we've finished with our other interviews."

"Actually," Graciela said, "would you give me your phone number and address again? I spilled coffee on your resume this morning and I can't read that information."

As Graciela was adjusting her notebook to write, Mr. Rigby's resume slipped out of the notebook and onto the floor. Mr. Rigby looked down at the remains of his resume and raised an eyebrow.

"That's a dark stain there," Mr. Rigby remarked suspiciously.

"Oh, I like strong coffee especially in the morning," Graciela said with a nervous laugh.

"That's quite a tear," Mr. Rigby observed about the paper. "Do you have a pet?"

"No, but I want a dog," said Emmanuel, who was always looking for a chance to bring up the topic.

"Quite," Mr. Rigby remarked expressionlessly.

Graciela handed him a blank sheet from her notebook where he copied down his information. They all rose and bid each other goodbye.

"Mr. Rigby," Emmanuel added as Mr. Rigby was turning to go, "I saw you drive into the parking lot with your green car. I think you should check the oil. Older cars need their oil checked quite often."

"Quite," Mr. Rigby remarked as he turned to leave.

Graciela sat down and let out a deep sigh.

"That didn't go very well," Graciela said. "We didn't make a very good impression on him."

"He didn't make a very good impression on us," Emmanuel said.

"What's going on?" Marshall asked as he picked up the mangled resume.

"Emmanuel had a little accident this morning," Graciela said. "Anyway, I'm sure Mr. Rigby is a wonderful classroom teacher for high school and university students.

But as a one-on-one tutor for Emmanuel, I don't think so."

"And I don't think Emmanuel's ready to read Tolstoy," Marshall said.

"Quite," Emmanuel said imitating Mr. Rigby.

The three laughed.

"He's not very fun either," Emmanuel added. "But he can be my tutor if you get me a dog, so I can have some fun."

"Emmanuel, we've been through this many times," Marshall said.

Emmanuel remembered his parents conversation from the night before and decided now was the time to make use of it.

"The dog could protect me," Emmanuel said. His mom said nothing, but her expression told him that his line hit close to her heart.

"Protect you from what?" Marshall asked, suspicious about where this thought came from.

"Oh, I don't know," Emmanuel said. "The dog could be my constant friend because I don't have any friends any more." Emmanuel was great at showing self-pity. Again, Graciela showed no expression but this line made her feel guilty.

"When was the last time you e-mailed Chauncy?" Marshall asked, trying to disprove Emmanuel's statement.

"Yesterday," Emmanuel said.

"And Grandma?" Marshall asked.

"Two days ago," Emmanuel said. "But it's not the same."

"You like to travel?" Marshall continued, acting like a lawyer with Emmanuel on the witness stand.

"Yes," replied Emmanuel the witness.

"You like adventure?" Marshall continued with the cross-examination.

"I haven't seen one yet," Emmanuel rebutted. "The only adventure I've seen is fractions."

"I'm sure our next case will involve more adventure," Marshall said. "This is new for all of us. We talked it over, the three of us, at great length. We're going to do it for a while and see if we all like it."

"What's a while?" Emmanuel asked.

"Six months, a year," Marshall said.

"A year?" Emmanuel whined. "That's seven dog years."

"You're not a dog," Marshall said.

"I don't want to *be* a dog," Emmanuel said. "I want to *have* a dog."

"You've made a commitment to try this out and we're going to try it out," Marshall said, getting the last word. "Once you show that you're good at commitments then maybe, just maybe, we can talk about the very big commitment of caring for a dog."

Just then, a woman in her mid-forties appeared at the entrance to the restaurant. She looked around as if searching for someone. She was wearing an off-white dress with a bright orange and yellow flower design on it. She had a matching scarf and an off-white purse. Her blonde hair was tied up in a bun. She had a look of confidence and a sense of mischief about her.

She walked right over to the McClue's table.

"McClue party of three," the woman said in her best imitation of a restaurant hostess.

"How did you pick us out?" Graciela laughed, somewhat surprised at the woman's playful way of greeting them.

"Not too many people of color in this London hotel," the woman said as she looked around, reinforcing that they were the only black and Hispanic people in the room.

"Yes, of course," Graciela said, "Ms. Jordana Jamison, please sit down."

"Emmanuel," Jordana said as she sat next to him. "You're much more handsome than I thought you'd be."

Emmanuel showed shock on his face. Graciela and Marshall laughed at his embarrassment.

"So, you want to learn to read," Jordana teased. "No, that's not right. Oh, I'm confusing you with my last student, a first grader. You want to read literature."

That was Jordana's way. She'd butter a person up with one charming line and then chop him down a bit with the next one. Either way one felt her affection.

"Wait a minute here," Graciela teasingly joined in. "Who's conducting this interview?"

"Sorry," Jordana said, "I'm not very good with following the proper way of doing things. I think I'm still rebelling against my proper British upbringing. Yes, yes, down to business now."

"Your resume is very impressive," Graciela began with her usual line.

"I think people shouldn't be impressive on paper," Jordana said. "They should be impressive in person. Right, Emmanuel?" She gave Emmanuel a little nudge with her elbow.

"Sure," Emmanuel said without really knowing what he was answering. He had not quite figured out Jordana. He did not think he would ever figure her out. Deep down, he liked it that way.

"What literature would you have Emmanuel read?" Graciela asked, covering the basic questions.

"I think that understanding any great literature comes from understanding the people from which it came," Jordana said, surprisingly giving a serious answer. "Wherever we travel Emmanuel would read the folk literature so he could feel the spirit of the people. If we went to Brazil, we'd read the folk tales there. If we went to Denmark, we'd read the fairy tales there. Then, we'd spend time with the people. We'd see the museums, sure, but just as important we'd get to know the people in the shops and on the streets. When Emmanuel is older and reads, say, Charles Dickens and Jane Austen, he'll be ready for them because he will understand the people from which they came. Dickens and Austen didn't write in a vacuum. They are thoroughly English. What does that mean? You have to find out. To understand James Joyce you must try to understand the Irish. A tough task. In Joyce's case you must understand all of classic mythology, too. There are layers upon layers, tradition building on tradition. It's a regular archaeological dig. Emmanuel, are you ready for an archaeology dig?"

Although Emmanuel did not understand everything she said, he was enchanted with this woman and found himself nodding, ready to start the adventure.

"Are you willing to travel?" Marshall asked.

"I've always traveled," Jordana said. "Why this year so far I've been in twenty-two countries and the year is young. But I'm reaching the age where I think it's time to pass on some of my travel knowledge to a deserving young person."

Jordana looked affectionately at Emmanuel.

"But I couldn't find any deserving youth," Jordana continued, "so I decided to teach Emmanuel instead."

Emmanuel laughed at the joke. Jordana definitely was a charmer. By the laughs and smiles on their faces, Graciela and Marshall were delighted by her, too. After the laughter died down, Graciela checked her notebook to see if everything had been covered.

"That's all our questions," Graciela finally said. "Do you have any questions for us?"

"Emmanuel, what are your hobbies?" Jordana asked.

"I like magic," Emmanuel said.

"Magic as in wizards and Harry Potter?" Jordana asked.

"Magic as in Houdini," Emmanuel said. "But I do like Harry Potter."

"I once ordered a magic kit when I was a little girl," Jordana said. "Three weeks passed and still it didn't arrive. So, I called the company. They said it must have disappeared."

Emmanuel found himself laughing at this woman who, in a matter of minutes, had swept him and his parents off their feet.

"Who do you work for?" Jordana asked, switching the subject.

"I don't know," Graciela said, obviously embarrassed.

"You don't know?" Jordana asked in surprise.

"We are not allowed to know the identity of our funder," Graciela said trying to sound reasonable.

"I call him Ben for short," Emmanuel said. "His full name is Ben E. Factor."

"Ben E. Factor," Jordana repeated slowly. "Oh, benefactor. I get it. Ha. Ha. Very good, Emmanuel."

"You've never met your boss?" Jordana asked.

"That's correct," Graciela said.

"And you're paid?" Jordana asked.

"Always on time," Graciela said.

There was a long pause. Jordana turned her head to look at Emmanuel then turned slowly back to face Graciela.

"Sounds smashing," Jordana finally spouted off. "I once had a boss who I wish I never met. He was so mean."

There was an awkward silence.

"C'mon Emmanuel," Jordana coached, "you know the drill. Let's try it again. My boss was so mean . . . . "

"How mean was he?" Emmanuel chimed in.

"He was so mean he had a sign on his desk that said, 'The Hospitality Stops Here,' " Jordana said.

Once again, Emmanuel laughed, taken in by the overflowing delight and silliness that came from Jordana.

"It was a true pleasure meeting you," Graciela said still laughing from the last silly line. "We will contact you as soon as we've made our decision."

"The pleasure has been mine," Jordana said in a straightforward manner with no teasing.

"I have your information here," Graciela said as she looked down at Jordana's airplane-folded resume to make sure it was readable.

The McClues rose to say goodbye and shake hands, then Jordana turned and left. Emmanuel quickly turned back to his parents as they all sat down.

"She's the one," Emmanuel said in a forceful whisper. "She's my tutor."

"Are you sure?" Graciela asked, wanting to make sure all the bases were covered. "We could interview more people in Boston."

"No, she's it," Emmanuel said more sure than ever.

Graciela looked around the table. Both Marshall and Emmanuel were nodding in agreement.

"Okay," Graciela said. "Jordana it is. We'll call her later from our hotel room and offer her the job."

The McClues left the restaurant. Emmanuel raced ahead to push the elevator button, but something caught his eye. He stopped in the middle of the lobby and a big smile came over his face. Through the glass of the hotel gift shop, he spotted Jordana trying on sunglasses. With each pair, she made a different expression. For one, she made a pouty expression. Another, a big teethy smile. Another, she stuck out her tongue. Emmanuel giggled at the clown show before him. He ran into the gift shop.

"Jordana," Emmanuel said. "You're my tutor. I mean . . . . "

"Oh, I'm sorry, Emmanuel," Jordana said, "I've just accepted a position tutoring this baby."

Emmanuel looked down. A baby in a stroller was grinning from ear to ear as Jordana continued making faces with the sunglasses.

"Just kidding, Emmanuel. Ha. Ha." Jordana chuckled.

Just then Graciela and Marshall came up.

"Emmanuel, you have to ask properly," Graciela said. "Sorry, Jordana. We would like to offer you the position. We hope you're interested. Will you accept?"

"Emmanuel," Jordana said, "I would love to travel the world with you, and I would love to travel through the world of literature with you. It will be my great pleasure."

Emmanuel stood there with no thoughts in his mind, just feelings of warmth with a hint of anticipation of the silliness, surprises, and adventure that would come from being with Jordana.

Ben E. Factor

EMMANUEL HAD THE WINDOW SEAT AS THEY FLEW OVER the Atlantic Ocean to Boston. Marshall sat in the middle seat and Graciela sat in the aisle seat reading a magazine.

"You'll have a lot of fun with Jordana," Marshall said. "You won't need a dog now."

"Are you calling Jordana a dog?" Emmanuel teased. "I'm telling."

"You know what I mean," Marshall said.

"I still need a dog," Emmanuel said.

"Why?" Marshall asked.

Emmanuel paused to think.

"To practice keeping commitments," Emmanuel said, trying to use Marshall's words against him. "It will help me grow up and become responsible."

"Oh brother," Marshall said, "I'm sorry I brought it up."

"You asked for it," Graciela said from behind her magazine.

"Emmanuel, it's time for our next theology lesson," Marshall said. "I think the assignment I'll give you today will keep you busy for most of the flight."

"What are we going to talk about today?" Emmanuel asked.

"The problem of evil," Marshall said.

Graciela jerked her head out of the magazine. She did not say anything but she kept an ear cocked. She knew he would not bring up the exorcism. At least, she did not think he would.

Marshall was trained by the Jesuit priests and brothers of Boston College High School and then Boston College. He thought of being a Jesuit for a while. He loved thinking through all the deep problems in his theology classes. Why is there a universe at all, instead of nothing? Where does evil come from? Does physics leave any room for God? Marshall also loved science and he was most interested in the questions that involved both science and religion. In the Jesuits, he could be a scientist and a priest at the same time. Marshall also loved Graciela and he wanted to get married, so he did not become a Jesuit. His current job was an answer to his lifelong prayers because it allowed him to do religion and science at the same time. He looked forward to having these lessons with Emmanuel so he could share these deep-thought puzzles that he so loved.

"Before we get started," Emmanuel said, "I have a puzzle for you."

"Are you stalling again?" Marshall asked.

"No, no," Emmanuel said, "it helps me get warmed up."

"Okay," Marshall said. "Shoot."

"What is the mirror image of God?" Emmanuel asked.

"The mirror image of God," Marshall repeated slowly as he pondered the question.

"Dog," Emmanuel said. "The word 'God' spelled backwards is 'dog.' "

"Enough," Marshall replied.

Emmanuel knew by his father's tone that it was time to stop fooling around. Marshall shifted in his seat then jumped right into the discussion.

"Why do bad things happen?" Marshall asked.

"I don't know," Emmanuel shrugged.

"Maybe Emmanuel is not ready for this," Marshall thought.

"Do bad things just happen or is there some evil force that makes them happen?" Marshall asked.

Graciela straightened up in her seat and gave Marshall the evil eye, so to speak. He was getting too close to talking about the demon.

"Maybe I'm not ready for this," Marshall thought, feeling his skin crawl. "This is not just some puzzle in a book. This is the reason we're running away from London. I don't want to scare Emmanuel with something I haven't faced yet."

With Graciela still staring at him, Marshall chose his next words very carefully.

"This is a 'bad thing' to talk about right now," Marshall laughed nervously at his weak pun. "Emmanuel, why don't you do what you were going to do."

Marshall felt himself sweating. He didn't realize until now how much the demon in London got under his skin.

"*That was weird,*" Emmanuel thought. "*I've never seen Dad like this before.*"

Emmanuel powered up his laptop computer and opened his word processor. He put his Dad's weirdness behind him as he began to type his e-zone thoughts and get them ready to e-mail to his best friend Chauncy. Emmanuel and Chauncy often talked to each other like they were stand-up comics.

> *Chauncy,*
>   *So what's the deal with middle names? What's up with them? Can someone explain these things to me? I found out what they're good for. My Mom yelled at me the other day and . . . .*

The McClue car was pulling into the driveway when Emmanuel woke up—kind of woke up. Emmanuel vaguely remembered getting off the plane, picking up his bags, and getting the car in long-term parking. The rest was a blur. Although it was only 9:30PM Boston time, the McClues were still on London time so it seemed like 2:30AM. The back door of the car swung open.

"Emmanuel," Graciela sang out. "We're home."

She poked him on the shoulder and shook him slightly. He moaned. She reached in and one by one pulled his feet out so they touched the ground. Then, she took his hands and helped him stand up. He looked like a boxer who was getting up after a knockout.

While Marshall carried the luggage inside, she led her zombie-like son into the house, up the stairs, and into his room. One end of the big paper banner over his bedroom door had come down. In blue marker, Emmanuel had written on the banner "Emmanuel's Kingdom." Kingdom? His room was more like a messy cave. Piles of books on the floor. Gadgets and magic tricks all over. Graciela did not like the mess. She had her limits. The bed had to be made everyday. The neat bed was an island in the clutter. She leaned Emmanuel against the wall, then hurried over to turn down the bed. She sat Emmanuel on the side of the bed then let him fall to the side so his head hit the pillow. Well, it almost hit it. Close enough. It seemed so long ago to her when Emmanuel was small enough to carry in her arms. This big lanky body was the same son she once carried in one arm. Hard to believe. She swung his feet one at a time onto the bed, then pulled off his shoes. Although she was a stickler for teeth brushing, she was not going to wake him to do that tonight.

"Good night, my dear Emmanuel," Graciela said. "May God keep you and protect you from all harm—and evil." She shuddered and pushed that thought out of her mind.

🐾   🐾   🐾

The poke-tickle-slap came just a few moments later. At least, it seemed that way to Emmanuel, but in reality it was nine hours later.

"We have to leave in thirty minutes," Graciela said, as she pulled off the blankets. "We have a meeting with our benefactor's lawyer."

Emmanuel did not remember any other wake-up calls, but all of a sudden the final warning had been reached with the poke-tickle-slap. This was not fair. You had to have a series of warnings where you could ignore the first few. That was the game. You could not start out with the final warning. His mom seemed serious and a bit nervous, so Emmanuel did not want to complain about the change of rules.

"Is it my birthday?" Emmanuel asked, confused by jet lag.

"Your birthday is in two days," Graciela said, as she pulled up the shades to get more light in the room.

"Can I go over to Chauncy's today?" Emmanuel asked.

"You'll see Chauncy tomorrow at church," Graciela said sensing stalling tactics. "Let's move!"

Emmanuel was up and moving to the shower before he realized he was wearing the same clothes he had on in London. He did the two-minute shower and dressed himself with the clothes that always mysteriously appeared on his bed when he returned from the bathroom.

He went to the kitchen. "*Is she ever going to let me grow up and pick my own clothes?*" Emmanuel thought, as he ate peanut butter and jelly toast standing up at the kitchen counter.

They arrived at the law offices of Downey, Chamberlain and Fox. Marshall was dressed in a navy suit and Graciela wore a business skirt and matching jacket. The waiting room was filled with brown leather chairs and couches. Emmanuel wandered around the room looking at all the wooden-framed diplomas and wooden-framed pictures of sailing ships that hung from the walls. Between phone calls and sips of coffee, the receptionist glanced suspiciously at Emmanuel above her black-rimmed glasses.

Finally, a woman with shoulder length, red hair and a sharp forest green business suit emerged from an office.

"Mr. and Mrs. McClue," Ms. Madeline Downey said, "please come in."

Emmanuel was left behind in the waiting room. He sat down on a long leather sofa. There were no sports magazines. He certainly could not take out his rubber ball here, not with the nervous receptionist eyeing him.

Inside Ms. Downey sat down behind her big oak desk while the McClues took their seats in front of it.

"Let's get right to the point," Ms. Downey said. "Your benefactor is very displeased by your decision to quit this case. You did not make a very good first impression. I have been asked to give you a warning: You are on probation. If you do not complete another case to the satisfaction of your benefactor, your funding will be cut off."

"I am very upset that our benefactor doesn't understand that the safety of our son comes first," Graciela said in a slightly angry tone. "We can protect Emmanuel from most human danger but not from the threat of spiritual evil."

"What about prayer as your protection?" Ms. Downey asked coldly. "Aren't you people of faith?"

"Are you a parent?" Graciela responded, ignoring the insult.

"Yes," Ms. Downey said.

"If a person who was possessed by a demon threatened your child what would you do?" Graciela asked.

"I am merely the messenger for the one who pays your salaries," Ms. Downey said. "You will be receiving your next case very soon. It will be a severe test of your abilities and will require the utmost secrecy. I hope you're up to the challenge. That will be all."

When they returned to the waiting room, Emmanuel was asleep with his feet on the leather couch under the irritated eye of the receptionist. As they left, she did not say anything. She let her stare do all the talking.

"How did it go?" Emmanuel asked groggily from the back seat of the car.

"Not very well," Marshall said.

Graciela was silent as she sat in the front seat with her arms crossed.

"So, 'Ben E. Factor' didn't give you a good grade," Emmanuel said, trying to make light of it. Graciela, however, was not in a joking mood.

"Now you know how it feels to get called into the principal's office," Emmanuel joked. "Why did we leave London early anyway?"

Emmanuel spoke without thinking. As soon as he said it, he wished he could have taken it back. There was an awkward silence. Then, Graciela suddenly turned around.

"Because it was too dangerous," she blurted. "I do not want to discuss this again."

"*What was so dangerous?*" Emmanuel thought. "*They were just investigating some teen who had special spiritual powers. At least, that's what they told me. I'll have to find out, but not by asking my parents.*"

There was silence for the rest of the ride home.

Speagle

"Jet lag," moaned a sleepy Emmanuel over and over again as his mother guided him out of his bed and into the bathroom.

"We're leaving for church in thirty-five minutes," Graciela said, as she closed the bathroom door with Emmanuel inside. Once she heard the shower running, she returned to his room and set out his clothes.

They drove into the school parking lot of St. Andrew's Catholic School. Emmanuel had not seen the long one-floor school building for several months. He attended the school from pre-school through fifth grade. When Graciela and Marshall started their new job he did not start sixth grade. All his friends still went there, including his best friend, Chauncy Phillips.

The church was one of the oldest in Cambridge. When they entered, the vaulted ceiling rose high above them. Carved figures seemed to come out of the walls. Stained glass let a rainbow of colors into the church.

The organ played as the McClues took their seats. Graciela and Marshall waved to friends. The opening song began and a long line of young people in white choir robes walked up the aisle holding their song books and singing. A drowsy Emmanuel suddenly became alert. He knew them all. There was Greg, Heather, Tamika, José, Leon, Alex, Mandy, Stanley, Hong, and Simeon. There was Paloma. Emmanuel had a crush on her. He never knew what to say to her. He just liked being in the same room with her. Kris, Lisa, Chantal, Catie, Arthur. There's Chauncy! Emmanuel used to stand next to him in the choir's second row.

How was he going to catch Chauncy's eye? When it was time to stand up for the Gospel reading, Emmanuel stood up just an instant before everyone else so Chauncy might notice him. During Mass, the congregation stands and sits several times, so Emmanuel had several chances to jump to his feet to get Chauncy's attention. But Chauncy did not notice him. Emmanuel's parents noticed, though. They gave each other a strange look. Emmanuel was usually one of the last ones to stand up.

Father Ferguson read the Gospel of Luke 9:37-43. Emmanuel spaced out, but the reading certainly got Graciela's attention. She broke out in a cold sweat. She could not help but think of the possessed boy back in London.

> *And behold, a man from the crowd cried, "Teacher, I beg you to look upon my son, for he is my only child; and behold, a spirit seizes him,*

*and he suddenly cries out; it convulses him till he
foams, and shatters him, and will hardly leave
him. And I begged your disciples to cast it out,
but they could not." Jesus answered, "O faithless
and perverse generation, how long am I to be
with you and bear with you? Bring your son
here." While he was coming, the demon tore him
and convulsed him. But Jesus rebuked the
unclean spirit, and healed the boy, and gave him
back to his father. And all were astonished at the
majesty of God.*

Hearing this passage, Graciela was so relieved that
Jesus was more powerful than any demon. She reminded
herself that this included the demon in London which
threatened Emmanuel.

Everyone sat down for the homily. Emmanuel stayed
standing for an extra second so he was the only one in the
church standing. Still, Chauncy did not notice him. Father
Ferguson started his homily. This was usually the time
when Emmanuel would go into the e-zone and stay there
quite a while. But something Father Ferguson said caught
Emmanuel's attention before he could slip into the e-zone.

"What is evil?" Father Ferguson said. "The boy in the
Gospel story is shaken and controlled by a demon. We usually think of evil as an earthquake that kills people. Or, we
think of evil as one person hurting another. But here, we
have a different kind of evil, a more direct evil, called a
demon . . . . "

"*Everyone is talking about evil these days,*" Emmanuel thought. "*My dad. Father Ferguson. Everyone except my mom, that is.*"

". . . Jesus can take on any demon," Father Ferguson said. "Rely on Jesus. Lean on Jesus. Pray to Jesus, always."

The homily ended. Nothing had worked to get Chauncy's attention, so Emmanuel tried holding his song-book a little higher in the air and waving it. That did not work either.

As communion started, Emmanuel got in line. He loved receiving communion. Receiving the host made him feel so connected to everyone in the church. He also felt so connected to Jesus and to God. Connected, that was the word. But he could not get connected to Chauncy. After receiving communion he walked in front of the singing choir. Emmanuel stopped for a moment and faced them. Suddenly, Chauncy looked up from his songbook and a huge smile broke over his face. Emmanuel continued back to his seat but kept looking back at Chauncy. Word spread through the choir like a wave. Without missing a beat in the song, the choir members nudged each other and pointed at Emmanuel. The whole choir was beaming a smile in Emmanuel's direction who beamed a smile back. At last, Emmanuel was really connected to everyone in the church.

After the last note of the final song rang out, the entire choir moved off the risers and swarmed around Emmanuel in his seat. A sea of white robes circled round him. Slaps on the back. Greetings. Handshakes. Paloma actually touched him on the shoulder and greeted him. He tingled all over.

Graciela and Marshall made their way out of the crowd of choir members, so they could greet their friends.

"How's the spy business?" Chauncy asked as he slapped Emmanuel on the shoulder and shook his hand up and down again and again.

"I've got an e-zone e-mail for you," Emmanuel said, returning a glowing smile.

Chauncy was the same height as Emmanuel and had slightly darker skin. They were both starting forwards on the fifth grade basketball team. They were called the "double digits" because they both averaged scoring about the same, and always in double digits. They had been best friends since the third grade.

"Can you come over today?" Chauncy asked eagerly.

"I'll check it out," Emmanuel said. "Come on."

Some of their classmates were leaving to go home, so the sea of choir robes dwindled as Emmanuel and Chauncy made their way over to Graciela and Marshall. The McClues were talking with Ralph and Marion Phillips, Chauncy's parents.

"May I go over to Chauncy's today?" Emmanuel asked.

Graciela looked at Marion Phillips.

"It's fine with me," Mrs. Phillips said. "It's great to see you, Emmanuel. You've grown as much as Chauncy has."

"We've missed you, Emmanuel," Mr. Phillips said. "I miss beating you in basketball in our backyard."

Everyone laughed.

"What's all the commotion here?" Father Ferguson asked, smiling as he approached the group. "Why,

Emmanuel, I should have known it was you. You always have a way of livening up a place."

The priest shook hands with everyone in the group.

"Marshall, Graciela, good to see you. You'll have to tell me about your new adventures," he said.

"Oh, we will," said Graciela as she gave her husband a knowing look. "Your homily hit a bit close to home."

"Don't they always?" teased Father Ferguson. "Look, I've got to keep moving. Give me a call."

An adult in a choir robe approached the group.

"Emmanuel," said Ms. Jennifer Campbell, the choir director, "so you're the reason the choir almost lost control during the communion song."

Emmanuel shook hands with Ms. Campbell.

"Emmanuel," Graciela said, "Dad and I are going to take Mrs. Phillips home, then go home ourselves. Mr. Phillips will bring you to Chauncy's house when you're through charming everyone here."

Graciela, Marshall, and Mrs. Phillips left. Mr. Phillips wandered off to a pew a little ways off and sat down to relax. Emmanuel heard a familiar voice come up from behind him.

"Emmanuel McClue. Good to see you," said the principal, Mrs. Debra Barry. "We miss you here, young man. I sure hope you enjoy traveling the world, but don't forget about us back here in Cambridge."

After Ms. Campbell and Mrs. Barry left, Mr. Phillips escorted the boys out to the minivan.

"Have to stop by the grocery store and get a few things," he said from the front seat.

The boys did not mind. They were chattering back and forth in the back seat, just happy to be together. They seemed to have their own little language filled with special phrases they used again and again. They spoke so quickly that hardly anyone else could understand them. It was as if they were downloading information to each other through a very fast modem. No one else's modem could keep up.

Mr. Phillips pulled into the grocery store parking lot and left them alone to catch up while he went into the store.

The boys did not talk about boring stuff like adults did. About his trip to London, Emmanuel did not talk about the weather, flight delays, and such. He talked about important things like throwing a paper airplane off the balcony, bouncing a rubber ball in a marble hallway, middle names, and that kind of stuff. Often they used many sounds when they talked. When describing a baseball game, they would not say, "At the crack of the bat, the runner ran to third and slid in just before the ball arrived." Rather, they would say, "Crack! Chug, chug, chug. Shoo. Safe!" Further, they would drag the sounds out. They might simply say "Crack!" Or, they might say "Craaack!" Or, they might say "Craaaaack!" Since they started e-mailing each other they developed a new way of typing these sound words. "Cra*3ck" meant "Craaack." "Cra*5ck" meant "Craaaaack." That way, they could make ridiculously long words like "Cra*4,569,832ck."

Regarding his paper airplane, Emmanuel did not say to Chauncy, "The plane nose-dived onto the aircraft carrier, then skidded off into the ocean." Instead, Emmanuel acted out the plane with his hand while he said, "Zo*24m. Cra*8sh. Ski*5d. Kabo*6m Spla*3sh."

"That's O. O. C." Chauncy said.

O. O. C. was short for "Out of Control." You actually said the letters so it sounded like "Oh Oh Sea." It meant something was extreme. The airplane crash was extreme in a good way, so, in this case, O. O. C. meant awesome or cool. O. O. C. could also mean something was extreme in a bad way. For example, if your teacher gave you too much homework or the principal gave you a detention, they were O. O. C. The boys even used their hand to sign the letters to each other across a crowded room.

Mr. Phillips returned with two bags of groceries and drove the boys to his home. Not once was Mr. Phillips able to enter into the conversation. Emmanuel and Chauncy were in their own little world.

The minivan pulled into the driveway. The boys hopped out and walked the front door, still chattering away.

"C'mon," Chauncy said leading the way, "I have something to show you."

Chauncy raced ahead into the living room. Emmanuel hurried behind.

"SURPRISE!" rang out a group of twenty people as Emmanuel entered.

Emmanuel was startled. He stood frozen taking it all in. The group broke out in the song "Happy Birthday." Most of the people he had just greeted in church were now standing in Chauncy's living room. Paloma and Catie pulled up a banner that said, "Happy Birthday Emmanuel." Others released the balloons they were holding and they rose to the ceiling.

"Busted," Chauncy laughed. "You were clueless. Gotcha. Spy boy just got duped."

Emmanuel, who had been talking non-stop in the car, was now speechless. He had not seen it coming at all.

"We're going to open the presents now because some of the girls have a skating party to go to," Graciela said after the song ended.

She led Emmanuel over to the far corner of the living room. Emmanuel sat down in the chair.

"Why don't you sit on the floor," Graciela suggested.

Emmanuel sat down cross-legged. From behind chairs and sofas emerged presents, big ones and small ones, all with ribbons. They were placed on the carpet at Emmanuel's feet. Flashbulbs started as Graciela and Mrs. Phillips recorded the event. Everyone else sat on the chairs and sofa, or else remained standing.

Emmanuel picked a small box and unwrapped it. It was a little flashlight.

"It's for spying around at night," Catie called out.

"Thank you, Catie," Emmanuel said.

He received a compass for finding his way and a scrapbook for placing pictures of his travels. Hong gave him a kit of fake mustaches, so he could disguise himself. Everyone laughed.

Lisa gave him a journal with kittens on the cover. Chantal gave him a pink neon pen to write in the journal. Some of the boys snickered.

"Thank you, Lisa. Thank you, Chantal," Emmanuel said. Inside, he was thinking that he would never use these things. They did not quite get the difference between a present for girls and a present for boys.

Chauncy gave him an advanced magic kit. Greg gave him a book about Houdini. Heather gave him an address book that had the addresses and e-mails of everyone in the class.

"Send us all postcards wherever you go," Heather said.

"Thank you, Heather. I will," Emmanuel said. Inside, he was thinking that there was no chance that would happen.

Mr. and Mrs. Phillips gave him a subscription to *National Geographic*. Graciela and Marshall gave him a nice backpack and some geography software for his laptop.

"Thank you, everyone," Emmanuel said. "I was really surprised."

"Surprised?" Chauncy said. "You were clueless. McClue was clueless."

Chauncy led a chant which all the kids joined, "Clueless. Clueless. Clueless."

The floor was covered with torn wrapping paper. Presents were all around him. The backpack was right in front of him. Emmanuel moved to get up.

"Stay right there, Emmanuel." said Graciela. "There's one more present."

All of a sudden, a beagle puppy bounded into the living room from the doorway.

"Ahhhhh," said all the girls.

The beagle sniffed at some of the torn wrapping paper. Then, it sniffed Catie's ankle. She giggled. The puppy spotted Emmanuel. Since Emmanuel was the person closest to the ground, the puppy took off and sprinted with its short little legs in his direction. Its floppy ears bounced up and down along the way. The puppy leaped over the backpack that was directly in front of Emmanuel. As it flew through the air, its long ears looked like wings sticking straight out on each side. It landed in Emmanuel's lap and climbed up to lick his face and neck. Emmanuel squirmed in delight.

"When did you get her?" an excited Emmanuel asked between the licks.

"Mrs. Phillips made all the arrangements," Graciela said.

"But you were both against a dog," Emmanuel said.

"We were just giving you a hard time," Marshall said.

"Dad, you were lying to me," Emmanuel teased.

"I wasn't lying," Marshall said. "I was acting."

"I didn't know you could act," Emmanuel said.

"What are you going to name her?" Graciela asked.

"She'll help me with my spy business," Emmanuel said.

"You need a lot of help," Chauncy said.

"She's a spy beagle," Emmanuel said, ignoring Chauncy. "Spy beagle. I got it! Speagle. Speagle the Spy Beagle."

"That's a cute name," Catie said.

"It's time for cake," Mrs. Phillips announced.

The girls moved in to pet Speagle. Emmanuel handed Speagle over to them. He stood up and moved into the center of the living room. In the midst of all this activity, Emmanuel disappeared into the e-zone for a moment.

"*Today was O. O. C.,*" Emmanuel e-zoned. "*Everyone is talking about evil these days. What about all the goodness?*"

"Hey, spy boy," Chauncy said, bringing back Emmanuel from the e-zone. "Want to go shoot some hoops in the backyard."

"Sure," Emmanuel said.

"We're having cake first," Mrs. Phillips corrected.

"Okay, later," Chauncy said. "My Dad wants a rematch in horse."

"Rematch?" Mr. Phillips asked. "I won last time."

"Yea, right," Chauncy said.

Emmanuel looked over at Paloma, who was holding Speagle. Lucky dog.

"Careful," Graciela said. "Here comes the cake with lit candles."

"We have to sing again," Mrs. Phillips said, who was carrying the cake.

"Happy Birthday to you," the group sang out. "Happy Birthday to you. Happy Birthday . . . . "

A New Case

EARLY THE NEXT MORNING, GRACIELA PULLED THE blankets off Emmanuel.

"Time to walk the dog," Graciela said.

"What?" Emmanuel groaned.

"You wanted a dog," Graciela said, "and this is part of having a dog."

"But it's my birthday," Emmanuel said. "Sleeping in is part of having a birthday."

"Emmanuel," Graciela said curtly.

Emmanuel knew that the argument was over. No logic was going to sway his mom, so he tried a different stall tactic.

"Thanks for the surprise party yesterday," Emmanuel said. "And most of all thanks for Speagle."

"You're very welcome," Graciela said. "Now, let's take care of Speagle."

She busied herself around the room while Emmanuel tried to get vertical. He sat up and reached for his sweats that were on the floor beside the bed. He slipped them on over his pajamas, then found some socks and tennis shoes to complete his outfit.

Graciela was excited. "We're flying to Italy today," she said, as she packed Emmanuel's suitcases.

"Is Speagle coming with us?" Emmanuel asked.

Adults would have asked a different question. What's our mission? How's the weather there? What part of Italy? What time are we arriving? But these things were not important to Emmanuel.

"Yes," Graciela said, "Speagle has her papers. She has her shots. We have a cage for her. She's ready to travel."

"So I'll have Speagle to play with on the plane?" asked an excited Emmanuel who got bored on the long flights.

"Not exactly," Graciela said, "Speagle will be in her cage in the cargo area."

"What!? She'll be scared down there all by herself." Emmanuel complained.

"Now you're worried about her," Graciela said. "You weren't worried about her a few minutes ago when I asked you to take her out for her walk. She'll be fine on the plane. Get going now."

Emmanuel headed out of the door in his sweats.

"The leash is on the kitchen counter," Graciela said. "Don't forget the pooper-scooper."

"Ugh," Emmanuel said.

Emmanuel made his way downstairs and into the kitchen. The kitchen table was covered with official look-ing reports. One report, which was opened to the middle, sat next to a cup of coffee. Emmanuel grabbed the leash and the scooper. As he entered the den, he heard some excited movement from the cage.

"Speagle!" Emmanuel exclaimed. "There you are in your mobile home."

Emmanuel opened the door and Speagle jumped out onto the crouching boy and licked his face.

"Did you like it when Paloma was holding you yesterday?" Emmanuel asked. "Tell me what it was like."

Emmanuel put Speagle to his ear. Speagle licked it and Emmanuel giggled.

"I thought it was nice," Emmanuel said.

He attached the leash and carried Speagle outside. The morning air was crisp. Emmanuel carried Speagle for about a half block before he remembered that she was supposed to take a walk. He set her down. Speagle darted around his ankles. Emmanuel had to lift his feet high over the leash that was constantly snarling at his ankles. Speagle became one curious nose that flitted here and there taking in whatever smelled interesting. *"Such a keen sense of smell will certainly be great for detective work,"* Emmanuel thought.

It looked like Speagle was walking Emmanuel. She romped from one smelly spot in the grass to another. Emmanuel could not get her to move until she was ready. Although they just walked around the block, it took almost a half hour to make the trip.

Speagle had no idea what a leash was. She walked on the wrong side of trees, fire hydrants, and street signs. The leash got hung up everywhere. Emmanuel tried to demonstrate that they had to walk on the same side of things, but it did not work. The only way to finish this walk was to follow Speagle's lead. She darted this way and that way around every obstacle on the street. Emmanuel followed. For the rest of the way, he made a game out of it, pretending he was downhill skiing around the flags on a mountain.

"How did the walk go?" Graciela asked, as she and Marshall were sitting at the kitchen table reading.

"Fine," Emmanuel said.

"Did Speagle go?" Graciela asked.

"Yes," Emmanuel said.

"Did you scoop it up?" Graciela asked.

"Yes," Emmanuel said.

He turned to the table. "What's all this?" he asked, pointing to the papers and reports.

"We are going to investigate the most famous relic in all of Christianity—the Shroud of Turin," Graciela said excitedly.

"A courier brought this packet early this morning," Marshall said. "It has tickets to Italy and all these documents about the Shroud."

"What's the Shroud?" Emmanuel said.

"It's a cloth that has mysterious markings on it of a man who was crucified," Graciela said.

"Many believe this cloth is the actual burial cloth of Jesus," Marshall said. "The markings were supposedly created when Jesus came to life during the Resurrection."

Graciela was ecstatic. "And we get to investigate it!" she said.

"So now you like Ben E. Factor?" Emmanuel asked.

"Better," Graciela said. "This case will make up for the last one that Ben gave us."

"What kind of markings are on the cloth?" Emmanuel asked.

"The markings are like the negative of a photograph," Marshall said.

"No one can explain how they got there," Graciela said. "No artist or scientist can reproduce the image."

"It's like having a photograph of the moment of the Resurrection," Marshall said.

"We'll tell you more about it on the plane," continued Graciela. "Our flight is at 6:30 tonight, but we're going to the airport earlier than usual because we've never taken a pet on a flight before, let alone through customs. Also, Jordana was supposed to arrive today. We didn't tell you because we wanted it to be a surprise on your birthday. We'll have to write her a note because it's too late to call her. Be ready to go right after lunch. Got it?"

When Graciela went into planning mode, she was an organizing freak. A steam roller with a calendar in hand. Emmanuel gladly left the room when she switched into this gear. He went back into the den, took out a tennis ball and bounced it. Speagle ran after it. If this is all Speagle and Emmanuel had in common, then they would get along fine. Emmanuel loved bouncing things around: basketballs, rubber balls. Speagle seemed to love it, too.

Two hours later, Emmanuel bounced the ball and it landed in Speagle's water dish inside the cage.

"Oh my gosh," Emmanuel said, as the water reminded him that he needed to get in the shower and get dressed.

He placed Speagle in the cage and got up. Speagle whimpered.

"I'll be back, Speagle," Emmanuel said. "Don't worry."

Emmanuel showered and put on the clothes that were set out for him on his bed. When he came downstairs for lunch, four large suitcases were by the door. The kitchen table was cleared of papers and set for lunch. They ate grilled cheese sandwiches and tomato soup.

Not ten minutes after the McClues drove off to the airport, a taxi filled to the brim with suitcases pulled up in front of the McClue house. Out of the back emerged a blonde woman in a knee length, white dress. The cab driver started carrying the nine suitcases and four garment bags to the door. Jordana rang the doorbell expecting a big welcome. She was ready to surprise Emmanuel on his birthday. She was also ready for a grand tour of this nice house. After she rang the bell, she noticed a manila envelope with her name on it. She opened it up and read the note.

Dear Jordana,

We are sorry that we are not here to greet you. This morning we were assigned to a new case. We're off to Italy. We're sorry we've been unable to contact you.

The key is in the envelope. Make yourself at home. Your room is the bedroom on the left at the top of the stairs.

Also in the envelope is flight information for flying to Milan and bus information for traveling to Turin. Take a few days to settle in before coming to Italy. Enjoy.

Sincerely,
Graciela McClue

Jordana tipped the cab driver, then opened the door and gave herself a tour. Nice functional kitchen. Cozy den. Spacious living room with rich carpet. She climbed up the stairs. She eyed the door to her room on the left, but wanted to snoop around a bit more before looking at her own room. On the right she saw the master bedroom. Peaking inside, she saw a perfectly made king size bed with a lush green comforter. A family picture sat on the dresser. Pictures of Emmanuel from different ages hung on one wall.

"What a cute baby he was," Jordana said to herself. "There's that smile already at such a young age."

A picture of Emmanuel in a bunny outfit. These are pictures that parents adore but children hate. "I bet Emmanuel closes this door when his friends visit," Jordana thought.

Jordana went down the hall farther and saw the banner over the door that read "Emmanuel's Kingdom." She pushed the door open and peered inside. "Wow! What a mess!" Jordana said. "More like 'Emmanuel's Pigpen.' " She quickly closed the door for fear of small animals escaping the room from beneath the piles on the floor.

At last, Jordana entered her own room. She immediately went to the closet.

"Not big enough," she thought. "I'll have to ask for more closet space. But, with a few touches of yellow and orange to brighten up the room, it could become my new pad."

Jordana began lugging her suitcases up the stairs to her room. After three trips with six to go, she decided to take a break and reward herself. She dragged the rest of her luggage inside, then pulled out the phone book to locate a good restaurant. Not one for cooking, Jordana located an Italian restaurant in Harvard Square. It would set the mood for her trip to Italy. Before leaving the house, she looked into the bathroom.

"Nice tub," she thought. "A good bubble bath would do me wonders." Jordana was very good at treating herself well. She called the restaurant for directions then headed down into Harvard Square for a fine meal.

The McClues were settled in their seats as the plane began the long trek over the Atlantic Ocean. Graciela and Marshall had their reports out. They were in heaven. Graciela read things of interest to a doctor. She read about all the wounds on the figure of the Shroud and how it matched the description of Jesus' death. Marshall read chemical reports on blood and the composition of the cloth. This was the perfect case for them. It brought together all their interests in medicine, chemistry, science, and religion. They chatted back and forth in scientific words when either found something of interest.

"*I wonder how Speagle is doing,*" Emmanuel e-zoned as he stared out the window. "*Maybe there are other dogs that she can talk to. Maybe there are cats that she wants to chase. I wonder how Jordana is doing. I can just imagine her arriving at our empty house. What a joke we played on her. Not on purpose. We could never outwit Jordana. I'll bet she'll get back at us somehow. I'll have to keep my eyes open for a practical joke from Jordana.*"

The Shroud of Turin

THE AIRPLANE LANDED, AND EMMANUEL WOKE WITH A start. His first thought was about Speagle. He could not wait to see her. As they walked through the airport, Emmanuel raced ahead to get to the baggage claim.

"Stay with us," Graciela said several times. "We're in a foreign country in a busy airport. Now, stay together."

In the baggage area, Marshall waited by the belt to pick up the regular baggage, and Graciela and Emmanuel went over to another door to wait for Speagle.

Some pet cages emerged. Two dogs were barking at each other. Speagle's cage was brought out. She joined in the barking. Speagle saw Emmanuel and put her front paws against the screen. She tried to lick Emmanuel's hands through the screen. Before Graciela could stop him, Emmanuel opened the cage and Speagle leaped out. Speagle took off and ran around the cages of the other dogs, and they went wild, barking and howling at Speagle. It was quite a scene. Emmanuel was chasing a little beagle puppy who was darting in and out of pet cages. Speagle ran between the legs of one owner. She was so happy to be free after several long hours in the cage. All the passengers waiting for their bags looked over to see what was causing all the noise. Marshall looked over—of course, Emmanuel had to be involved. Marshall hesitated. Should he rush over to help? Part of him was embarrassed that his son was causing the scene, so Marshall stood there for a moment and pretended that he did not know the young boy who was chasing the puppy.

To Speagle it was a big game. She would let Emmanuel get close and then take off again. Graciela came along with the leash. She could not grab Speagle, either. Finally, Marshall came along carrying two of their suitcases. He used the suitcases as a wall to block Speagle's path. That slowed her down enough so Emmanuel could grab her. Graciela came along a moment later and hitched the leash to the collar. When the McClues looked up everyone in the baggage area was looking at them. Some thought it was funny and had smiles on their faces. Others had scowls. Marshall grabbed their other two bags off the moving belt, and Graciela got a cart. They loaded up their bags and left the baggage area with as much dignity as they could muster.

Graciela tried to scold Emmanuel but in fact she thought it was funny. She was afraid that if she tried to say something she would break out laughing, so she said nothing.

Once on the bus to Turin, Emmanuel sat next to the window. Speagle stood on his lap with her front paws on the window. Emmanuel enjoyed watching Speagle stare out at the Italian countryside. When she saw some cows, she barked. Emmanuel tried to cover her mouth and turn her attention away from the window.

"Emmanuel," Marshall said, "we're going to see the Shroud of Turin this afternoon, and we want to tell you more about it."

Marshall sat next to Emmanuel and Graciela sat in the aisle seat. Emmanuel knew this was important and tried to listen, but Speagle kept squirming around in his lap.

"So, this cloth—called a Shroud—covered Jesus' dead body and now has special marks on it," Emmanuel said.

"Many people believe it covered Jesus' body," Graciela said.

"Why do they think it was Jesus' body?" Emmanuel asked.

"It has markings on it like no other burial cloth in the world," Graciela said. "Other burial cloths have stains from the decomposing body, but the Shroud has no decomposition marks."

"The Shroud has an image of an entire body laying there," Marshall said. "As I said before it's like a photograph."

"The body in the Shroud was only there for 24 to 36 hours," Graciela said. "If it would have been there any longer, the cloth would have had decomposition marks."

"What other evidence do you have?" Emmanuel asked, proud of his detective-like question.

"Pollen found on the cloth is consistent with the area of Jerusalem in the time of Jesus," Marshall said.

"Also, little insects called mites found on the cloth are consistent with the same time and place," Graciela added.

"There appear to be Roman coins placed over the eyes that date back to the time of Pilate, the same time as Jesus," Marshall added.

"All the wounds on the body are consistent with the Crucifixion," Graciela said. "There are nail wounds on the wrists and feet. The side was pierced with a lance. There are many small cuts on the head as if he were wearing a crown of thorns. Everything is consistent with the description of Jesus' death given in the Bible. Even the legs weren't broken. Usually, Roman soldiers broke the legs so the people hanging from the cross died quicker. With their legs broken, they could not support their bodies to breathe and so they would suffocate. It says in the Bible that Jesus was already dead so the soldiers didn't break his legs."

"If you have all this evidence why doesn't everyone believe that it was the Shroud of Jesus?" Emmanuel asked.

"Some don't want to believe that Jesus really existed," Marshall said, "so they create other explanations. Some say an artist faked the markings on the cloth."

"Is it possible?" Emmanuel asked.

"No," Graciela said, "no artist or scientist has been able to reproduce the image. They don't know how it was made."

"It wasn't a painting," Marshall said. "There are no paints, dyes, or pigments on the cloth. There are no brush strokes."

"How do you think it was made?" Emmanuel asked.

"There was a very rapid aging of the Shroud's topmost layer," Graciela said. "It was a sudden burst of heat or light that caused the scorch-like markings."

"Most believe that it was a high intensity burst of light lasting only milliseconds," Marshall said. "The body in the Shroud radiated intense light all over for just an instant and left marks on the cloth. The cloth is a photograph of the moment of Jesus' Resurrection."

"I can imagine light bursting out of every pore of Jesus' body as he came back to life," Emmanuel said. "O. O. C."

Emmanuel drifted off in the e-zone for a moment imagining this wonderful scene, but he snapped himself out of it as he tried to maintain his detective state of mind.

"Is there any evidence you've overlooked?" Emmanuel asked.

"There is one important thing," Graciela said. "In 1988, scientists tried to test how old the cloth was by a test called Carbon-14 dating. The test came back that the Shroud was dated between the years 1260 and 1390. This is the only test that says the cloth was not from the time and place of Jesus. Everything else points to Jesus."

"What do you make of this?" Emmanuel asked.

"Since then scientists have had trouble with Carbon-14 tests working very well on cloth," Marshall said. "For example, they would date a mummy and get a certain age. Then, they would date the cloth that the mummy was wrapped in, and the cloth would be much, much younger."

"The thinking now is that Carbon-14 testing doesn't work very well on cloth," Graciela said. "Cloth is easily contaminated. It has to be cleaned in certain ways before it can be tested."

"I think that the Carbon-14 testing of the Shroud is inaccurate. When scientists know how to test cloth better or come to the conclusion that cloth won't give accurate results, then all the evidence will point to the Shroud as the burial cloth of Jesus," Marshall said.

"What are we going to investigate about the Shroud?" Emmanuel asked.

"First, we're going to be able to see it with our own eyes," Graciela said. "That's a great honor. We were told that we'd be given further instructions after we saw the Shroud."

"Old Ben E. Factor is playing games with us again," Emmanuel said. "Ben leads us around."

"Just like Speagle leads you around," Graciela said as she pointed at Speagle. "I saw you trying to walk Speagle yesterday morning. It was so funny."

"You don't think it's funny when Ben leads us around," Emmanuel said.

"Ben's our new boss," Graciela said. "It will take a little while to get to know each other. Just like you and Speagle, we need some time to get to know each other."

"We can't get to know Ben," Emmanuel said. "We don't even know who Ben is. Who do you think Ben is?"

"Ben must be very rich and well-connected," Marshall said.

"But why is Ben doing this?" Emmanuel asked.

"Ben might believe in God but wants some proof," Marshall said.

"Or, Ben might not believe in God and wants us to disprove all the miracles we come across," Graciela said.

"Don't you want to know who Ben is?" Emmanuel asked.

"A little," Marshall said, "but I want to study miracles and Ben gives us the money to do it. I want to study miracles more than I want to know who Ben is."

"Well, I want to know who Ben is," Emmanuel said. "Ben could be our greatest mystery of all and I'm going to find out who he is."

"Tell us if you find out anything," Graciela laughed.

"I want you to save all the mailings you get from Ben," Emmanuel said.

"They come from Ben's lawyer, Madeline Downey," Graciela said.

"Maybe she's Ben," Emmanuel said.

"She's never seemed interested in what we do," Graciela said.

"It's all an act," said Emmanuel.

"I don't think she's rich enough or powerful enough," Marshall said. "It took a pretty powerful person to get us over to London to work with Roger Thigpen."

"We're not talking about that again," Graciela insisted.

Marshall and Emmanuel looked at each other and shrugged. The conversation was over. Speagle finally settled down and rested in Emmanuel's lap. Emmanuel stared out the window at the beautiful Italian countryside. "*I'll figure out who Ben is,*" Emmanuel thought. "*I'll just keep collecting the clues.*"

When they arrived in Turin, they got off the bus and took a taxi to the hotel. They brought their bags to their room and then ate lunch in the hotel restaurant. Speagle stayed in her cage in the room and ate her dog food. After lunch, they took another taxi to the home of the Shroud, the Cathedral of St. John the Baptist. They rang the bell of the large house next to the Cathedral.

A middle-aged, round man with thick black hair answered the door. He was wearing a black robe that was tied around the waist with a rope belt.

"You must be the McClues," he said in good English but with a thick accent. "I am Father Anthony Moriconi. Very happy to meet you."

He reached out and put his right hand on Marshall's shoulder and his left hand on Graciela's shoulder. He looked like he was giving Graciela and Marshall a half-hug.

"You are investigators from America," Father Moriconi said. "Welcome to you."

Father Moriconi then spied Emmanuel.

"You must be Emmanuel," Father Moriconi said. "Nice name. Do you know what it means? Of course, you do. I am to show you our beautiful Shroud. One moment please, while I get my keys."

Father Moriconi had done all the talking. But he was so friendly that Graciela and Marshall did not notice that they had yet to say a word. It was a nice greeting.

Graciela was very excited. She had read all about the Shroud. She had seen pictures of it in books, but now she was going to see it in person. A tingle ran up her spine.

Father Moriconi returned with a big ring of keys dangling from his hand.

"Little doggie," Father Moriconi said, looking down at Speagle. "I am sorry but you cannot come with us. Father Dominic will take you for a walk. Would you like that? Of course, you would."

An eighty-year-old, thin priest took small, shuffled steps as he slowly made his way to the door. Father Dominic's gray hair was slicked back and thinning. He did not speak English. He did not even try. He just smiled. Father Moriconi did all the talking which was no surprise.

One look at Father Dominic and Graciela did not know if he could handle Speagle. Father Dominic did not look very sturdy as he shuffled along. Speagle could easily wrap the leash around his leg and trip him.

"I don't think...," Graciela said, trying to suggest a new idea for Speagle.

"Little doggie and Father Dominic will have fun together," Father Moriconi said. "Right, little doggie? Of course."

"But, but...," Graciela persisted.

"Let us go now," Father Moriconi said.

He handed the leash to Father Dominic. Smiling, Father Dominic shuffled off down the sidewalk. Speagle ran this way and that. She ran ahead until the leash was tight, then she ran back until the leash was tight. Father

Dominic kept moving along at a slow, steady pace. Father Moriconi led the McClues over to the side door toward the back of the Cathedral. Graciela kept looking back at Speagle and Father Dominic. They were moving along with no problems yet. Maybe Father Dominic's legs were so close together as he shuffled that Speagle could not get between them. Graciela took one last look, said a little prayer for Father Dominic, then went through the side door as Father Moriconi held it open.

It was dark inside the Cathedral. The only light came through the colored stained glass. It was quiet and beautiful. The click of their shoes on the marble floor echoed off the walls. Father Moriconi led them across the back of the church, and opened another door that led down a spiral staircase to the basement.

The basement had a low ceiling, and Marshall had to be careful not to hit his head. They came to a series of locked metal gates. Emmanuel counted five of them. Father Moriconi approached a priest who sat by the first gate.

"We always have someone watching over our Shroud," Father Moriconi said. "We didn't used to have all these gates, but strange things have happened. About fifteen years ago, an odd group of men in dark blue suits broke in. They didn't hurt the Shroud, but now we are more careful."

The two priests nodded to each other. Father Moriconi unlocked the first gate. The McClues went through. The basement was dimly lit. They seemed to be walking toward ever greater darkness. Clang. The gate slammed behind them. Emmanuel jumped. Creak. The second gate was unlocked and opened. They walked closer to the darkness at the end of the hallway. Clang. The second gate locked behind them.

Father Moriconi did not speak. He became more serious as they moved closer to the dark area at the hallway's end. Creak. Clang. Creak. Clang. There was no turning back now. There were four locked gates behind them and only one before them. The final gate made a long, slow creak as Father Moriconi swung it open. They stepped inside. Father Moriconi released the gate and it slammed behind them.

"Stay here, please," Father Moriconi said.

The McClues huddled next to each other. Emmanuel did not know what to expect. A pitch black area loomed before them. Father Moriconi's heels could be heard clicking over to the right side. No more steps. Total silence. Total darkness before them. Emmanuel could hear his mom's nervous breathing. She reached out and grabbed Emmanuel's hand.

In the next moment, they heard the switches of a breaker box clicking into place. Several spotlights blazed in an instant. The McClues covered their eyes. There it was! Their eyes adjusted to the bright light. Completely encased in glass was a large piece of cloth fourteen feet long and almost four feet wide. The McClues were six feet from the cloth and from there the ghostly image of a bearded man with long hair and closed eyes appeared in the cloth.

Graciela gasped and fell to her knees. She was no longer a scientist studying this cloth; she was a believer adoring it. Marshall's mouth dropped open. Emmanuel felt a chill run through his body. This cloth could have touched Jesus. This could be a picture of the moment when Jesus came back to life. Emmanuel felt his knees become weak.

They stared without speaking. Three minutes later the timers on the spotlights counted down and the spotlights shut off. The cloth faded back into the darkness.

Father Moriconi escorted them back through the gates. They walked out in silence. They were changed people—seeing and believing for themselves.

"You can take a longer look tomorrow," Father Moriconi said. "I understand a Shroud expert will be here with you."

The McClues could not talk as they left the Cathedral. Even though Father Moriconi was giving them time to talk, they were so amazed they were speechless.

"Now let's get your little doggie," Father Moriconi said as he went into the rectory to find Father Dominic.

Father Moriconi came out a few minutes later.

"Father Dominic hasn't come back yet," Father Moriconi said.

"Oh my goodness," Graciela said. "I bet Speagle tripped him."

The McClues and Father Moriconi split up to search. Marshall and Father Moriconi looked around the outside of the rectory. Graciela and Emmanuel walked around the Cathedral. Graciela imagined poor Father Dominic falling on the sidewalk with Speagle licking him trying to help him. She took off running. Emmanuel followed.

When Graciela and Emmanuel reached the other side of the Cathedral, they saw two figures in the distance. Emmanuel ran toward them. It was Father Dominic and Speagle. Father Dominic was smiling and shuffling along. Speagle was being Speagle, darting this way and that. They both looked fine. Father Dominic walked so slowly they had not made it around the block yet.

Graciela was relieved. In Italian, she said "thank you" to Father Dominic over and over. Father Dominic smiled and nodded. Emmanuel took Speagle's leash. The four of them slowly made their way back to the rectory where they met Marshall and Father Moriconi.

The McClues thanked both priests again, waved goodbye, and caught a cab back to the hotel. Still amazed by the Shroud, they did not say a word to each other the whole way back.

Argentina!

"Emmanuel, Emmanuel," Marshall said, shaking his son's shoulder. "Time to get up."

"What?" moaned Emmanuel, still half-asleep.

His dad never woke him up. It was always his mom's job. Something must be wrong.

"Another packet was delivered from Ben E. Factor about an hour ago," his father said.

"An hour ago?" Emmanuel groaned. "What time is it?"

"It's six o'clock in the morning," his father answered.

"Where's Mom?" Emmanuel asked.

"She's out taking a walk to cool down," Marshall said. "She's very angry about this. She was so looking forward to studying the Shroud."

"What happened?" Emmanuel asked.

"We have orders to catch a flight to Buenos Aires, Argentina later this morning," Marshall said. "All it says is that we will get further instructions when we arrive there."

"Ben is really playing games with us," Emmanuel said. "Is Mom ready to quit working for Ben?"

"She was," Marshall said, "but we talked it over."

"I didn't hear any yelling," Emmanuel said.

"We can talk things over without yelling," Marshall responded.

"If Mom's angry she can't stop herself from yelling," said Emmanuel.

"Okay, we took a walk and talked it over so Mom could raise her voice," his father said.

"She's really going to let Ms. Downey have it when we get back to Boston," Emmanuel said.

"Maybe there's something even more mysterious waiting for us in Argentina," Marshall said.

"That's my dad, always looking on the bright side," Emmanuel said. "What's more mysterious than the Shroud?"

"I don't know," Marshall said.

"Did that argument work with Mom?" Emmanuel asked.

"No, you need to get moving. We have to catch the seven o'clock bus back to Milan so we can make our flight."

As Emmanuel sat up in bed, Graciela came back in the room.

"If Argentina doesn't give us a great case we're quitting," Graciela announced. "I'm tired of being led around the world on a wild goose chase."

There was no arguing with Graciela now. Emmanuel quickly slipped into the shower. Marshall quietly finished packing. He knew better than to discuss things with her when she was like this.

They barely made the seven o'clock bus. A playful Speagle kept Emmanuel entertained on the trip.

"We can't call Jordana now," Graciela said as they arrived at the airport in Milan. "It's the middle of the night in Boston. We'll have to call her once we land in Argentina."

They said goodbye to Speagle at the baggage area. The McClues boarded their flight and prepared for take off.

"*I'm going to be a total zombie without Speagle,*" Emmanuel thought. "*We're going to arrive in Buenos Aires, Argentina tomorrow morning at six o'clock. We'll be on the plane for about a day. Can you actually die from boredom?*"

Emmanuel became so bored he finally took out his pre-algebra book and started working on fractions. Marshall and Graciela kept reading reports on the Shroud.

"There must be some connection between the Shroud and Argentina," Marshall said.

"When Ben's lawyer said that this case would severely test us," Graciela said, "I didn't know she meant our patience."

When they finally landed, Emmanuel's legs were numb and he could barely stand. It was a two-hour wait for the bus to Bariloche. Emmanuel played with Speagle, tossing his rubber ball for her to fetch. Graciela called Jordana in Boston but no one was home, so she left a message.

"I wonder where Jordana is," Graciela said. "I hope she didn't take off for Italy. I'll call the hotel there."

The bus ride took another six hours. Then, they took a taxi, which took forty-five minutes to reach their hotel. Emmanuel felt like he had aged thirty years on the trip. His joints were stiff and his bottom was numb.

They pulled up to a five-story hotel nestled in the mountains. During the winter, it was a ski resort. During the summer, people came to enjoy the beautiful weather and to go hiking.

When the taxi pulled up, a boy about Emmanuel's age wheeled up a cart and helped the driver unload the luggage from the trunk. The boy came around as the weary McClues climbed out of the cab.

"*Bienvenidos*," said the boy. "My name is Joshua. My parents run this hotel."

Joshua spoke in Spanish. Of course, all the McClues understood. Joshua had olive skin, dark brown hair, and soft brown eyes. He was about three inches shorter than Emmanuel. Emmanuel, who was so tired from the trip, suddenly got a burst of energy when he saw Joshua.

"Do you want to go swimming?" Joshua asked Emmanuel.

Emmanuel turned to his mom. "Can I Mom?" he asked excitedly.

"This is the most life I've seen in you since we left Italy," Graciela said.

"Can I Mom, please?" Emmanuel asked.

"Yes, after we get the luggage to our room," Graciela said.

Emmanuel put Speagle on top of the luggage on the cart, then got behind the cart and, with Joshua's help, raced it towards the door.

"Easy," Marshall called out.

When the cart reached the door, Emmanuel turned and ran back to Graciela.

"Can Speagle go swimming, too?" Emmanuel asked.

"Does Speagle know how to swim?" asked Graciela.

"Sure she does," Emmanuel said. "Well, we'll teach her if she doesn't."

"If it's all right with Joshua's parents," Graciela said.

"Great!" Emmanuel exclaimed, as he turned to run back to the door.

Marshall paid the taxi driver. By the time Graciela and Marshall reached the front desk in the lobby, Emmanuel had the key in his hand and was holding the elevator door open with the cart. Joshua was standing by his side.

"Come on, hurry up," Emmanuel said.

"We have to sign in and pay for the room," insisted Graciela.

"It's all taken care of," said Emmanuel. "You know, the Ben Factor."

"We'll see about that," Graciela said. "You go on ahead. We'll catch up."

"Mr. and Mrs. McClue," began Mrs. Ramirez, the co-manager of the hotel. "Room 403 is ready for you. We have been expecting you."

"I think your son and our son have become friends already," Graciela said.

"Oh, yes," Mr. Ramirez said. "They will have a lot of fun together here."

"And your name is?" Marshall asked.

"I am Juan Ramirez," Mr. Ramirez said. "This is my wife Maria. Joshua is our foster child. We have no children of our own."

"Joshua has been with us for thirteen months now," Mrs. Ramirez added. "He seems to like it here. We love him dearly. And we can certainly use his help around here."

"You must be very tired from your travels," Mr. Ramirez said. "Why don't you go to your room and rest."

"There is a Mr. Clemente who's been asking for you," said Mrs. Ramirez. "He asked us to tell him when you arrived."

"We don't know a Mr. Clemente," Graciela said. She gave Marshall a puzzled look.

"He's reserved a private conference room for a meeting with you tonight," Mrs. Ramirez said. "But first you must settle in and get some rest."

As Graciela and Marshall reached their room, Emmanuel bolted out of it wearing his swimming suit with a towel draped around his neck. Speagle was on her leash running along beside him.

"Emmanuel, wait!" Graciela said.

Emmanuel stopped in his tracks.

"Be very careful with Speagle," Graciela ordered. "And don't you go in the water unless there is a lifeguard on duty."

"Yes," Emmanuel said.

"Where did you get all that energy?" asked Graciela.

"I thought I was going to die of boredom on the trip," Emmanuel said. "Joshua is the answer to my prayers."

Emmanuel and Speagle turned and ran off down the carpeted hallway.

"I've never seen him go from being so tired to so excited," Graciela said. "Maybe all this isn't good for him. He needs kids his own age."

"This trip almost did us all in," Marshall said. "I wouldn't have made it through the trip if I didn't have the Shroud to read about."

Marshall sat on the edge of the bed. He took off his shoes and rubbed his sore feet. "The pool sounds pretty good right about now," he said.

The phone rang in the hotel room.

"Hello," Graciela said. "Mr. Clemente . . . Yes, we had a safe trip. I see . . . Sure, we could meet . . . That would be fine . . . First floor conference room . . . Room 101C . . . See you in a few minutes . . . Goodbye."

"The pool is going to have to wait," Graciela said to Marshall. "We're going to find out why we came here. And it had better be good."

Marshall stopped rubbing his feet and put his shoes back on. On the way down to see Mr. Clemente, Graciela and Marshall made a detour to the outdoor pool. They saw Speagle diving into the shallow end of the pool after the rubber ball that Emmanuel had thrown in. Speagle's ears stood straight out as she flew through the air. Her short little legs paddled over to the ball as her long ears floated straight out on each side of her head. Joshua swam under her and popped out of the water right beside her. But nothing distracted Speagle from retrieving her rubber ball. She got it in her mouth and swam back toward the side. Emmanuel tried to get it from her but she would not release her bite on it until Emmanuel lifted her out of the water and set her down on the side of the pool. Then, she dropped the ball. Emmanuel picked it up and threw it back into the water. Speagle dove again and the fetching process started over. Even the lifeguard was enjoying the little show.

"I thought Emmanuel was training Speagle," Marshall said. "Looks like it's the other way around."

Graciela and Marshall left the pool area and found the group of conference rooms on the first floor. The door to Room 101C was slightly ajar. They pushed their way in to find a huge wooden table that could easily seat thirty people. A round-faced, slightly overweight, gray-haired man in a light blue suit sat at the near end. He rose when they entered.

"Have a seat Dr. Marshall and Dr. Graciela McClue. I am Dr. Miguel Clemente," Mr. Clemente said very formally.

The three sat in chairs around the near end of the table.

"So, why are we here?" Graciela asked.

"Because your benefactor wanted you to be," Mr. Clemente answered.

"We know that," Graciela said.

"You wouldn't be here if I had my way," Mr. Clemente said.

"You don't want us here. We don't want to be here," Graciela said. "Fine. We'll go back to the Shroud."

"Soon you won't want to go back," Mr. Clemente said.

"Studying the Shroud is a dream come true for us," Graciela said.

"The Shroud is just an old piece of cloth," Mr. Clemente said.

"You don't believe in the Shroud?" Graciela asked.

"I believe in the Shroud more than you do," Mr. Clemente said.

"I'm confused," Graciela said.

"I believe in what the Shroud can do," Mr. Clemente said.

"What it can do?" Graciela asked, puzzled.

"What do you think of the boy?" Mr. Clemente asked.

"Don't change the subject," Graciela said.

"What do you think of the boy?" Mr. Clemente persisted.

"Joshua?" Graciela asked. "He seems like a nice boy. Emmanuel certainly likes him. Look, we didn't travel all this way to find a playmate for Emmanuel."

"Certainly not a playmate," Mr. Clemente said. "How about a savior?"

"What?" Graciela asked.

"The Shroud pales in comparison . . . ," Mr. Clemente said.

"To what?" Graciela interrupted.

"To whom," Mr. Clemente corrected.

"I don't understand," Graciela said.

"Joshua is the Shroud come to life," Mr. Clemente said.

Marshall spoke up for the first time. "Are you saying what I think you're saying?" he asked. "Joshua is a clone of the person on the Shroud?"

"Exactly," Mr. Clemente said. "Joshua is made from genetic material on the Shroud."

"A clone of Jesus?" Graciela exclaimed.

"Many people would say that," Mr. Clemente answered.

There was a stunned silence.

Mr. Clemente pushed a stack of reports across the table toward the McClues.

"It's all right here," Mr. Clemente said. "I am forced to turn all of this over to you. Here are the records of the cloning process and a detailed history of Joshua's life. Joshua doesn't know who he is. He will be told when he's eighteen. You must keep it a strict secret."

"And who are you?" Graciela managed to blurt out at last.

"I'm not your mysterious benefactor, if that's what you think," Mr. Clemente said. "Let's just say that I'm responsible for the well-being of Joshua. We'll meet again tomorrow morning after breakfast. I'm sure these reports will keep you more than busy until then. They must remain locked in this room. Here's your key."

Mr. Clemente tossed a key to Graciela. The three rose from their chairs. Graciela and Marshall headed out of the room followed by Mr. Clemente, who locked the door with his key.

Graciela and Marshall headed back to the pool, each deep in thought. Their trip to Italy and their sudden trip to Argentina now made some sense. These two distant parts of the world were two pieces of the same puzzle. But there were so many missing pieces.

They came out to the pool area to find Emmanuel and Joshua resting on pool chairs with Speagle lying close by. They could not help but stare at Joshua. Who or what was he?

As soon as Emmanuel saw his parents, he raced toward them.

"Joshua wants to take me camping with him tomorrow," Emmanuel said. "Overnight camping in the mountains. Can I go? Joshua is an expert camper. Please."

Graciela and Marshall could not manage an answer. Graciela just kept seeing Joshua as the boy Jesus. One moment she felt that she was back in time two thousand years. The next moment she felt that the boy Jesus had jumped ahead two thousand years. She felt light-headed.

"I'm not feeling so well," Graciela said. She sat down slowly and carefully in a pool chair.

"We'll talk about it later, Emmanuel," Marshall said. "The traveling has worn us out. We've got to get some rest."

As the evening sun set in the mountains, Marshall helped Graciela walk slowly back to the elevator. A demon, the Shroud, now this. What would be next?

Joshua

Jordana stared out the window of the bus as it neared the town of Turin. She wanted to surprise the McClues, so she did not call ahead of time. She had found a great book of Italian folk tales that she would use as her first reading book with Emmanuel. In order to understand the literature, you must understand the people. That was Jordana's ideal. Jordana certainly had studied the people of Cambridge during her short time there. She remembered back to her short stay in Cambridge where she had treated herself to some of the best restaurants, a different cuisine for each meal: Mexican, Italian, Thai, and American pizza. She fondly remembered the coffee shops and book stores.

The bus pulled up to the Turin bus station. Jordana claimed her luggage and flagged down a cab. Any cab driver was going to have to work hard. Three heavy suitcases and two stuffed garment bags sat on the sidewalk. Of course, Jordana thought she was traveling light.

On the way to the hotel, she tried to think of something clever to say when a surprised Emmanuel answered the hotel room door. "Here's your homework, special delivery," she thought. Then she would hand Emmanuel the Italian folk tale book. That would be good.

At the hotel, she approached the desk and asked in perfect Italian for the McClues. The clerk checked their records, but there was no one there by that name. Jordana insisted. The clerk checked again, then got the manager. The manager remembered the McClues and handed Jordana a fax the hotel had received.

> *Dear Jordana,*
>
> *We missed each other again! We are very sorry. We called Cambridge but you must have already left.*
>
> *We were in Italy for only one day before we were sent to Argentina. Below you will find all the information to find us there.*
>
> *You can either return to Boston to wait for us, or you can come to Argentina. Emmanuel looks forward to seeing you again. Also, our new dog, Speagle, will love you.*
>
> *Enjoy Italy while you're there. Hope to see you soon.*
>
> *Sincerely,*
> *Graciela McClue*

"Trying to surprise the McClues always backfires on me,"

Jordana thought. "Oh well, let's see what Turin has to offer."

She checked into the hotel and drew herself a hot bath. Later she would find a good bookstore and, of course, a good restaurant.

By the time Mr. Clemente entered Conference Room 101C the next morning, the McClues had already been there for two hours reading the reports on Joshua. They had read through about one-third of the stack. Mr. Clemente took a seat at the end of the long table.

"Joshua is only twelve and he has had eighteen different foster homes," Graciela said. "Why?"

"Very perceptive," Mr. Clemente said. "We knew that Joshua would need to be moved occasionally. . . . "

"Occasionally?" Graciela interrupted. "Eighteen times in twelve years?"

"We raised Joshua to speak Spanish," Mr. Clemente said. "That gave us a wide range of countries that he can move to. He's starting to learn English. That will give us even more countries where he can live. Look, as scientists I thought you would be interested in the marvels of cloning."

"We'll get to that," Graciela said. "As a medical doctor I'm also interested in the overall well-being of Joshua. You are avoiding my question. Why does he need to be relocated so often?"

"We never planned it this way," Mr. Clemente said. "We thought we might have to move him two or three times. But they are so persistent."

"Who are they?" Marshall asked.

"Every Christian would love to meet Joshua," Mr. Clemente said. "In fact, they would come in flocks and droves to seek him out."

"And you didn't anticipate this?" Marshall asked.

"Of course we did. We've done a great job of keeping the secret."

"But why has he been moved eighteen times?" Graciela persisted.

"Imagine you belong to a group that thinks the cloning of Jesus is the Second Coming," Mr. Clemente said.

"So, some group knows about Joshua, and they think the end of the world is about to happen," Marshall said.

"Yes," Mr. Clemente said. "The group is called *La Segunda Venida.*"

"The Second Coming," Marshall translated.

"What do they want with Joshua?" Graciela asked. "Do they want to hurt him?"

"No, they believe Joshua can save them from harm at the end of world. They want to kidnap him and have Joshua among them for protection," Mr. Clemente said.

"You weren't aware of this group?" Marshall asked.

"We were, but we didn't know how persistent and resourceful they were. They've been chasing us around the world," Mr. Clemente answered.

"How close are they?" Graciela asked.

"We think we have a month or two before they find us again," Mr. Clemente said.

"Why did you try to make a clone of Jesus?" Marshall asked.

"If you were to pick one person in history that you wanted to clone who would you pick?" Mr. Clemente asked. "For me, it was Jesus."

"I said try to clone Jesus because we don't know for sure if the Shroud of Turin is actually the burial cloth of Jesus," Marshall said.

"Making a clone from the genetic material on the Shroud will be another way to test it," Mr. Clemente said. "We'll meet the person who was buried in the cloth."

"But you won't meet the person," Graciela said. "A clone is an identical twin of the person, not the same person. Joshua is not Jesus."

"Strange—yesterday, Mrs. McClue, you seemed to believe. You became pale and unusually quiet when I told you who Joshua was," Mr. Clemente said.

"It boggles the mind to think that Joshua might be the clone of Jesus. But, after I thought it through, I see the truth. Clones, like identical twins, will have the same genetic material. They will look alike. They will share some of the same personality traits, likes and dislikes, but that's all. They are different people."

"That's what Joshua will help us test," Mr. Clemente said. "Jesus had some abilities that we are beginning to test Joshua for. We will see if clones share deeper abilities than just looks and personality."

"What do you mean?" Marshall asked.

"We are currently testing to see if Joshua has the ability to heal people. We put a number of sick people in Joshua's presence. Some know who he is. Others do not, so we have a test group. We want to see if anybody gets better when they are around Joshua."

"Won't Joshua get suspicious with all these sick people around?" Marshall asked.

"People often come to this resort area for the nice weather. We just tell him that the nice weather here is good for their health." Mr. Clemente said.

"Won't the people who know tell Joshua who he is?" asked Marshall.

"So far, no one has. We tell people that if they tell they will have to leave immediately. Besides, if someone told you that you were Jesus, would you believe them?"

"But Joshua doesn't know that he might have healing powers. Jesus willed people to be healed." Marshall said.

"We know. When Joshua becomes eighteen and is told who he is, we'll then see if he can really develop any healing powers. For now, we want to see if his compassion for the sick generates any healing."

"Are there any results yet?" Marshall asked.

"It's too early to tell. Part of the agreement to let you come here is that you, Mrs. McClue, would use your skills as a doctor to examine the people to see if any healing is taking place."

"It's possible that people will feel better because they believe that Joshua is Jesus," Graciela said. "It's like taking a sugar pill. If you think the sugar pill is real medicine then you might feel better."

"That's why we have two groups. The group that doesn't know who Joshua is, and the group who does," Mr. Clemente said.

"Joshua is being treated like a lab rat in a big experiment. He is a human being. He deserves his own life. He is not just an experiment," Graciela said.

"I resent what you are saying. I have been overseeing Joshua's care since before he was born. I have planned out every detail. He is like a son to me. I have seen that he has been given the best of everything. So don't tell me that he is being treated like a lab rat."

"But he is not Jesus. He is a clone!" Graciela insisted.

"Perhaps. But science and time will show us how close to Jesus he actually is." Mr. Clemente said. "I think our meeting is done for now. We have covered none of the science. I hope you will soon get over all these initial questions, so we can get down to the marvels of science that you have been given the privilege of witnessing. Good day."

Mr. Clemente rose from his seat and left the room.

"This is scary," Graciela said, as soon as the door closed. "One moment he acts like Joshua's proud father. The next like an objective scientist."

"Let's take a break and find Emmanuel," Marshall said.

Graciela and Marshall found Emmanuel in the day care room that looked out onto the pool. Joshua, Emmanuel, and Speagle were playing with some young children there. Mrs. Parra was in charge of the day care, but Joshua stopped by everyday to play with the children, most of whom were between the ages of five and eight. Joshua was very good with young children. He liked to organize little soccer games at the far end of the room. He would play goalie and roll out six to eight little plastic balls, and all the children would kick their ball. It was a madhouse with balls flying everywhere. The children would try to kick the balls between cones set up as a goal. Joshua dove this way and that, rolling on the floor to stop the shots. The children would laugh and laugh as Joshua's body flailed around playing super-goalie. Emmanuel joined in and together with Joshua they played double goalie. Emmanuel and Joshua hammed it up as they pretended to bump into each other and knock each other down going for the same ball. Speagle, too, joined in chasing after any balls that came her way. When she caught one, she would race around and not give it back. Emmanuel would have to chase her to retrieve the ball.

Maripe, a nine-year-old, watched the action from her wheelchair. She giggled as the two clown goalies tumbled this way and that. When the soccer game was over, Joshua brought over a mini-basketball to Maripe. He wheeled her over to a plastic basketball hoop that was about six feet off the ground. Maripe took a shot and nearly made it. Soon, all the other children picked up their soccer balls and came over. The soccer balls became little basketballs, and Joshua and Emmanuel now tried to block their shots. They goaltended right and left, swatting the little plastic balls across the room. The children screamed with delight and chased down their balls, so they could shoot again. The shot-blockers had to leap over Speagle who was always trying to get a loose ball. Finally, Speagle got tired of nearly getting stepped on, so she went over to Graciela and Marshall where it was safe.

When Maripe shot, Joshua and Emmanuel never blocked her shot. One of the boys would get her rebound and bring it back to her. Maripe kept her eye on Joshua. Even when Emmanuel brought her ball back, Maripe didn't say much or seem to notice him. She only had eyes for Joshua.

"I bet she's been told who Joshua is," Graciela said to Marshall.

"Or, she has a crush on him," Marshall said.

"Maybe both," Graciela replied.

The couple enjoyed watching the two boys put on their clown show. It was hard to believe that this normal acting twelve-year-old boy was the source of so much controversy and that he was not even aware of it.

Emmanuel spotted his parents across the room and ran to them.

"Are you having fun?" his mother asked.

"Oh yes," said Emmanuel, breathing hard. "Joshua and I are going to help Mrs. Parra serve lunch. And, this afternoon we want to go camping. Can I go?"

"Where are you going to camp?" Marshall asked.

"Up on the mountain. Joshua knows all the best campsites," Emmanuel said.

"How long will you be gone?" Graciela asked.

"We'll only go overnight," Emmanuel said.

Graciela and Marshall exchanged glances.

"Yes, you can go. Before you leave, make sure you talk to us again. Understand?" Graciela said.

"I understand," Emmanuel said. "Thank you."

Emmanuel ran back to Joshua just in time to catch one of the shots and slam dunk it. Soon all the kids wanted the boys to dunk their shots. Alley-oops followed alley-oops with most of them unsuccessful. Emmanuel lifted one of the boys up, so he could dunk it himself. Soon all the children wanted to be lifted to make slam dunks. Speagle ran back over to the group and chomped down on a loose ball. Emmanuel picked her up and held her mouth over the basket. Speagle dropped the ball through the hoop and everyone cheered. By the time each child had a few turns, Emmanuel and Joshua ran out of energy. Mrs. Parra saved them by calling for lunch. Mrs. Parra had even prepared a lunch for Speagle. Joshua and Emmanuel served the kids their food, then got their own lunches and sat with Maripe. Maripe's big brown eyes stared dreamily at Joshua, but Joshua did not seem to notice.

After lunch, Joshua and Emmanuel left the day care with Speagle and went to the storage room where they packed their backpacks. Emmanuel had never been camping before. Neither of his parents was the outdoor type. *"This is going to be a great adventure,"* Emmanuel thought. He had read *The Swiss Family Robinson* and imagined surviving in the wilderness, but he had never actually tried it.

They packed two backpacks. Joshua carried the tent

and a sleeping bag in his backpack. Emmanuel carried a sleeping bag and the kitchen supplies in his backpack. There was a skillet, pan, knife, plates, cups, and eating utensils. Besides that, they both carried headlamps, matches, mosquito netting, rain ponchos, and some dried snacks. They walked into the kitchen and Joshua snooped through the big refrigerators for food to cook for that night's supper and the next day's breakfast.

They wore their backpacks as they walked through the lobby of the hotel with Speagle in tow.

"Have fun Emmanuel," Mrs. Ramirez said. "Joshua is a great camper. Don't worry about a thing."

Still wearing their backpacks, the two boys took the elevator to the fourth floor to talk to Emmanuel's parents. Graciela laughed when she opened the door and saw the two large backpacks.

"When will you be home tomorrow?" Graciela asked.

"Tomorrow afternoon," Emmanuel said.

"Joshua, Emmanuel has never been camping before so you're in charge. Emmanuel, listen to what Joshua tells you," Graciela said.

"You're embarrassing me, Mom."

Emmanuel walked across the room and dug through a drawer for his toothbrush and a couple extra shirts. He dug a bit deeper and pulled out his compass. He turned around too quickly and bumped into a lamp with his backpack. Graciela straightened the lamp and gave him a big hug with her arms extending around his backpack.

"You're embarrassing me, Mom," Emmanuel said again.

After the two boys left, Graciela and Marshall went to Conference Room 101C to read some more. An hour later, Mr. Clemente came to the conference room door.

"Do you know where Joshua is?" he asked with some urgency.

"He and Emmanuel went camping overnight," Graciela said.

"*La Segunda Venida* is narrowing in on us," Mr. Clemente said.

"But you said it would be a month or two," Marshall said.

"They must been getting better at tracking us," Mr. Clemente said.

"How long do we have?" Marshall asked.

"It could be today. It could be a couple days. I don't know." Mr. Clemente said.

Camping

JOSHUA, EMMANUEL, AND SPEAGLE CROSSED A TREELESS area that was a ski run. They walked under a large tower that supported the cable and chairs for the ski lift and then they disappeared into the woods.

"Can't we just take the ski lift up?" Emmanuel asked. "That could save us a couple hours of walking."

"That's cheating. Besides, we're just cutting across as we head away from the ski runs," Joshua said.

After a few minutes in the dense woods, Emmanuel looked back and could not see the run or the ski lift towers.

"Do you really know where you're going?" he asked.

"Yes," Joshua responded. "I have marked five trails that are my favorites. We're on the star trail right now. See?"

Joshua pointed to a tree on the right and there was a small star etched into the trunk about a meter off the ground. Every seventy meters or so, Joshua pointed out a new star on a tree that they passed. The stars were small enough so that they would not be noticed unless they were being looked for. But for someone who was aware of them, they were like street signs marking out a sure, straight path through the forest.

Joshua led the way. Speagle was on her leash but she was getting better about walking on the same side of the trees as Emmanuel, so they did not get hung up.

They reached a babbling brook. *"It really does sound like it is talking, or babbling,"* Emmanuel thought. The clear water raced along spilling over rocks.

"I have to rest," Joshua said. "I don't know what's wrong with me today. I usually walk all the way to camp with no problem."

Joshua was sweating. He took off his pack and sat down on a rock by the stream. He drank from his water bottle. He coughed several times. Speagle drank from the stream while Emmanuel made sure she did not fall in.

"You have other trails marked?" Emmanuel asked.

"I find places I like to camp and I mark trails to them," Joshua said. "There are trails marked by squares, triangles, circles, and crosses. The circle trail is my favorite, it leads to a cave."

Joshua got up and coughed a couple more times, then drank some more water.

"To cross this brook we have to go up upstream about twenty meters," Joshua said.

Once again he took the lead. He crossed the brook stepping on large stones that were just below the surface of the water.

"Be careful," Joshua warned. "The rocks can be slippery."

Emmanuel walked across carefully. Speagle jumped in and swam while Emmanuel kept her leash tight so the water would not carry her away.

"What do we do?" Graciela asked Marshall and Mr. Clemente.

"The boys have an hour lead on us," Marshall said. "We're not going to catch them."

"We can't just sit here and do nothing," she persisted.

"Joshua knows these mountains better than anyone," Marshall said. "We're not going to find them. And if we're not going to find them, then that radical group, *La Segunda Venida*, is not going to find them, either."

Graciela paced around the room then turned to Mr. Clemente.

"You keep us up to date on *La Segunda Venida*!" she commanded.

Joshua, Emmanuel, and Speagle picked up the star trail and continued on up the mountain. After forty-five minutes, Joshua took another rest. As they got higher, it got cooler. Each boy put another shirt over the one he was wearing to get a layered effect.

"This is embarrassing," said Joshua, as he coughed again. "A city boy comes to the mountains and I'm the one asking for breaks."

After another forty-five minutes, the wind started picking up. The sun disappeared behind a very dark cloud.

"Something's moving in," said Joshua. "It will probably blow over quickly."

The boys put on their rain ponchos and continued climbing. The first lightning strike came unannounced in the distance.

"One, two, three...," started Joshua. "...thirteen, fourteen, fifteen, sixteen."

CRA*8CK!!!

Emmanuel ducked. Speagle whimpered. Some big drops of rain pelted the hoods of their ponchos.

"Five kilometers away," Joshua said.

"What!?" Emmanuel exclaimed.

"When you see the lightning you start counting," Joshua said. "When you hear the thunder you divide by three to get how many kilometers away it was."

They continued walking for a few more minutes. A few small flashes in the sky, then another ground strike.

"One, two, three...," started Joshua. "...seven, eight."

CRA*10CK!!!

"Wow! It's less than three kilometers," Joshua said. "It's moving fast. It's time to get in the lightning position. Do what I do."

The big drops were coming harder now. Joshua took off his backpack and set it on the ground, he moved a few steps away from it, then squatted down as if he was a baseball catcher. Only the rubber soles of his hiking boots touched the ground. Emmanuel did the same thing.

"Now make sure your heels are touching," Joshua instructed. "That way, the lightning that comes up through the ground will go up one of your rubber soles then arc back down the other one into the ground. It won't go into your body. Keep those heels touching and don't touch the ground with anything else."

Emmanuel picked up Speagle and held her in his lap so she was off the ground.

"The next one is going to be close," Joshua said.

They waited like that for a few minutes. Their legs began to ache from the awkward position. The rain came harder.

"Now I know what it's like to be a catcher," Emmanuel groaned.

A light flashed. It seemed to flash all around them at the same time.

CRA*14CK!!!!

No time between flash and sound. Speagle howled, but Emmanuel could barely hear her among the deafening rumble. It was as if God had whipped the earth right beside them.

"Stay in position," Joshua ordered.

The next two lightning strikes got farther and farther away. The storm had rolled over them in a matter of minutes. Shaken, Emmanuel stood up. Again, Joshua led the way. The blood flow returned to their legs. The big drops lessened, and in another couple minutes the rain stopped.

"Awesome!" Emmanuel yelled.

Speagle was still shaking, so he held her in his arms.

"Nature never disappoints," Joshua said, as they removed their ponchos.

The two boys and a scared puppy continued up the mountain on the star trail.

"Look at that storm," Graciela said, as she and Marshall stared at the rain and lightning on the mountain.

"Joshua knows what to do," Marshall said.

Graciela began to pray. "Dear God, please be with Emmanuel and Joshua, and protect them from all harm and all evil." she said.

The boys and Speagle finally reached the campsite. Joshua was very tired and coughed every few minutes.

"I don't know what's wrong with me," he said.

"Don't worry," Emmanuel said. "My mom's a doctor, and she'll check you out when we get back down."

"I'll gather wood for the fire while you set up the tent," Joshua said.

"I've never set up a tent before," Emmanuel said.

"I'll get you started," Joshua replied.

They took off their backpacks and Joshua took the tent out of his. It was amazing that the tent could fold up to be so small. Joshua showed Emmanuel how to put the poles through the slats in the tent, then went off to gather wood. It was going to be dark in about a half an hour, and they needed to get the fire going. Emmanuel concentrated to get all the flexible poles through the slats. A domed tent formed before him. He set it on its rubber pad and then went off to help Joshua with the wood. Speagle saw Joshua collecting wood, and she picked up a stick, too. The boys laughed.

"The trick is to get wood of different sizes," Joshua said. "We need underbrush and moss to get it started. We need twigs and sticks to keep it going and bigger pieces to get it roaring."

"Everything is wet," Emmanuel said.

"It will make it harder, but we can do it," Joshua replied.

They returned to the campsite with armfuls of different sized pieces. Speagle dragged along a thin, short branch so as to do her part.

"A campsite is set up in a triangle," Joshua explained, as they came into the open area. "Our fire is in one corner of the triangle. We store the food in another corner. The tent is in the third corner."

Joshua stopped and looked around.

"Emmanuel, where's the tent?" he asked.

They both looked around, then dropped their wood and ran around to search.

"It was here," Emmanuel said, standing on the rubber pad.

Joshua laughed. "I forgot to tell you to stake it down," he said. "It blew away. Let's search downwind."

Joshua took off running while Emmanuel and Speagle followed. They ran for about fifty meters before they spotted it caught between two trees. It was very light and a gust of wind caught it and sent it sailing farther. The chase was on. It was like trying to catch a homework paper when it's dropped on the playground. Just when it seems ready to be caught, a gust of wind shoots it off again. Speagle barked at it because it seemed to have a mind of its own. Finally, Emmanuel grabbed a corner. Speagle grabbed the same corner and growled. Joshua moved in to get another corner.

They pulled the tent back against a swirling wind. If they had a string tied to it, it would have made a great kite, except it would have gotten caught in every tree. The tent struggled to get loose, but finally they got it back to camp where they put it on its rubber pad and staked it to the ground.

From where they were, they could see the hotel down below. The two boys stopped to look and ponder.

"I often come up to about this spot when I need to get away," Joshua said. "When I think my problems are so big, I come up here, look down on the hotel, and see that my problems are really very small. This is God's view of the hotel."

Emmanuel stood in silence and imagined his parents down there with his mom probably worrying about him. Joshua was right. It was very peaceful to see things from way up here.

Compared to the tent, the fire was pretty easy. They had to block the wind with their bodies as they tried to get it started. Because of the dampness, it took longer to get the initial underbrush going, and it was dark by the time the fire was started. They had to be careful not to smother it when they added each new batch of larger pieces. Because of the wetness, the fire snapped and popped when the larger logs were put on. Speagle acted as if she thought it was alive. She barked, growled, and circled the fire like it was a threat to her. Of course, the boys encouraged her fantasy.

"Get it, Speagle," Emmanuel said. "Come on, go after it."

A large pop sent a small cinder flying Speagle's way. Hitting the ground in front of her, she sniffed it. The hot cinder touched the end of her nose. She yipped, drew back in pain, and ran away whimpering.

"Poor Speagle," Joshua said.

"Oh, Speagle," Emmanuel said, as he ran into the dark after her.

Cra*3sh. Thu*3d.

"Are you all right?" Joshua called out.

"I'm fine." Emmanuel's voice came from the darkness.

He emerged from the dark limping slightly with a tear in his pants. Speagle was in his arms. They put her nose in water. That's all they had to cool her burn. It was tiny but it probably stung. Emmanuel continued to hold her, so she would not play around the fire.

"What's for dinner?" Emmanuel asked. "I'm starving."

"An American classic," Joshua said. "Hot dogs and baked beans."

Joshua boiled water for the hot dogs. The baked beans sputtered in their pan. Beans flew out. Speagle almost jumped out of Emmanuel's arms to check them out but then thought better of it and stayed where she was.

The American meal tasted very good. It was a nice surprise for Emmanuel. It made him feel welcome and at home. After dinner, they dug a hole and washed their plates, pans, and silverware so that the water ran into the hole. They filled in the hole when they were finished. Joshua placed the remaining food in one of the backpacks, then swung a rope over a high branch on a tree. He tied the rope to the backpack and hoisted it up so that no animals could reach it from the ground or from the tree.

"Where we store the food is the third corner or our camp triangle," Joshua said. "Do you want to sleep outside?"

"You mean after all that with the tent, we're not even going to use it?" Emmanuel asked.

"If it rains or gets too cold we will," Joshua said. "But I love to sleep under the stars. Once the fire dies down you won't believe the view."

They pulled out their sleeping bags and placed them on rubber pads. They put on their head lamps, turned them on, and climbed into the sleeping bags. They looked like miners. Speagle snuggled up on the rubber pad by Emmanuel's sleeping bag. They turned towards each other with their head lamps and blinded each other. Both boys giggled.

They turned off their head lamps and settled down for

the night. The fire died down, and the stars became spectacular. It was like the theater lights dimming then the curtain opening to reveal an awesome stage.

"I never knew there were so many stars!" Emmanuel exclaimed. "In Boston, you can barely see them. Hey, the stars are all messed up. The constellations! They're all messed up."

"In the Northern Hemisphere the constellations are at different angles than they are here," Joshua said.

"I feel like I'm on a different planet," Emmanuel said.

"No, you're just on a different part of this planet," Joshua said.

"Have you ever lived in the Northern Hemisphere?" Emmanuel asked.

"Yes," said Joshua, "I've lived in Mexico, Guatemala, Costa Rica, the Dominican Republic, Spain...."

"Wait a minute," Emmanuel interrupted.

"I've had eighteen foster families," Joshua said.

"Why so many?"

"I have no idea," Joshua said. "My case worker, Mr. Clemente, keeps recommending that I move."

"With no explanation?" Emmanuel asked.

"Not really," Joshua said, "just stuff about my different foster parents not adjusting well."

Across the darkness, Emmanuel could sense that Joshua was crying.

"I'm sorry," Emmanuel said.

"I think things are going well and then all of a sudden I'm moved again," Joshua said, as he wiped away his tears.

"I'm very sorry," Emmanuel said.

There was a pause, then Joshua changed the subject.

"I love to come up here though," Joshua said. "I feel like I can reach up and touch the heavens. Sometimes I've tried to connect all the stars together like a big connect-the-dot book. If I could do that I would get the face of God. What else could I possibly get? Up here, I even feel close to my real parents. They were killed in a car accident when I was a baby. But up here, I talk to them."

"Do they talk back?" Emmanuel asked.

"In a way," Joshua replied. "I feel things in my heart. I feel their love. I feel like I see the big picture."

"You certainly do," Emmanuel said, as he motioned to the universe above them.

"You know what I mean?" Joshua asked.

"I know exactly what you mean," Emmanuel said.

The two boys chatted some more, then drifted off to sleep on a mountaintop with a million stars above them.

Secret Revealed

THE FULL MOON SHONE DOWN ON THE SLEEPING TRIO of two boys and a dog. A sky full of stars watched over them. Suddenly, a dense fog swept over the mountaintop. It curled around the trees and descended on the sleeping bags. It absorbed all sound. There was nothing but silence. It absorbed all light, and there was nothing but the pitch of black. The moon and stars were gone. The fog pressed down on them like a heavy presence. Emmanuel woke up. Everything seemed closed in on him. He felt like he was sleeping in a coffin. He reached to turn on his headlamp, but it would not light. He reached out to search for Speagle and Joshua. His arm fought against a pressure as it tried to reach out. He felt nothing around him. Suddenly, he felt he was moving, gliding across the ground but not touching it. He opened his mouth to cry out but the fog-like stuff was like cotton filling his mouth. No sound came out. Then, it was heard, seemingly coming from everywhere and nowhere at the same time. In a deep, nasty voice, "Think he's safe? Think again!"

Graciela sat straight up in bed. She was sweating and panting. What a nightmare! She hurried to the window to look up at the mountain. A beautiful full moon and a canvas of stars on a clear night loomed above her. She wiped the sweat off her face. She looked back to her bed. Marshall was still asleep. Those nasty words, which she first heard in London, still echoed in her head. Where did demons go after they were exorcised and were forced out of the person they possessed? Was the demon now in Argentina pursuing Emmanuel?

Then it dawned on her. "Evil needs people to do its work," she thought. "The demon in London needed Dennis to scare us. I shouldn't be afraid of evil in general or a demon. I should be on the watch for people who are doing bad things, cooperating with evil. The scary thing about this place is that everybody thinks they are doing the right thing. Mr. Clemente thinks it is good to clone Jesus. He thinks it is good to lie to Joshua about his real parents. Now, he thinks it is good to do tests on Joshua. *La Segunda Venida* thinks it is good to kidnap Joshua so they can be close to him. Forget about the demon. Watch out for people doing bad things. That's the way to protect Emmanuel from evil."

With that thought, Graciela felt some calm come over her, so she climbed back in bed. Marshall was still sound asleep. Graciela looked out at the mountain one more time, said a short prayer to Jesus for protection, and rolled over beneath the covers.

After breakfast, Graciela took a chair from the pool area and set it up behind the hotel so she could watch the mountain. She kept staring at the forest by the ski runs, and imagined a dog and two boys bounding out of the forest. She stayed there all morning and waited.

"It's lunch time, dear," Marshall said, as he walked up behind her.

"I'm not leaving this spot until they come back," Graciela said. "What have you been doing all morning?"

"Reading reports," Marshall answered.

"I can't concentrate enough to read," Graciela said.

Just then, a small animal came bounding out of the forest onto the ski run. Graciela jumped from her chair. A few seconds later two figures with backpacks emerged. Graciela ran a few steps forward, then stopped.

"I don't want to appear too anxious," she thought.

The boys were chattering back and forth. Speagle was darting around this way and that, completely free of the leash. The boys saw Graciela and Marshall and waved from a distance. Graciela and Marshall returned a big wave.

"Welcome back," exclaimed Graciela with open arms and a big smile as she reached to hug her son.

Emmanuel saw the worry in his mother's face. Behind her forced smile was something else. "*It can't just be the camping,*" Emmanuel thought. Emmanuel fell into his mother's hug. She grabbed on tight and held on for a few seconds too long. Something was indeed wrong.

"Did you have a good time?" Graciela asked, as she looked her son over. "You ripped your pants."

"I fell once," admitted Emmanuel. "We slept under the stars. We cooked over a fire. It was awesome. We want to go again in a few days. Can we?"

"Maybe," Graciela said, trying to maintain her fake smile.

"Joshua has a cough. Would you check him out?" Emmanuel asked.

"It's nothing," Joshua said.

He coughed several times.

"You see," Emmanuel said.

"You made me think of coughing," Joshua said. "It's the power of suggestion."

"Yeah, right," Emmanuel said. "You were coughing the whole trip."

"I'll check you out after lunch," Graciela said. "Why don't the two of you shower up? It smells like you could use it. Then, we'll have lunch together."

Graciela and Marshall came up to their room to freshen up for lunch as Emmanuel was finishing getting dressed after his shower. Speagle was sleeping in her cage.

"Feel better?" Graciela asked Emmanuel.

"Yeah," he said.

"Smell better," Graciela teased.

"Very funny," Emmanuel responded. "Mom, Dad, why are we here? I'm having fun with Joshua, but what are we doing here? You didn't just come here to read reports in a locked room. What's going on?"

Graciela and Marshall were caught off guard. They had not talked over what to tell Emmanuel.

"And Mom, you seem worried about something," Emmanuel continued. "You have the same look on your face that you had in London. You wouldn't tell me anything then. Are you just going to keep secrets from me? Is this what your work is all about? Secrets?"

"Emmanuel, sit down," Marshall said. His mind wrestled with what to say and what not to say. "We have some things to tell you. We didn't know why we were sent here until Mr. Clemente talked to us the day we arrived."

"Are you sure this is all right?" Graciela asked.

"Yes. If Emmanuel knows, he can help us protect Joshua," Marshall answered.

"Protect Joshua from what?" Emmanuel asked.

"Emmanuel," began Marshall, "Joshua is in danger of being kidnapped. For his whole life . . . . "

"That's why he's had eighteen different foster homes," Emmanuel interrupted.

"He's been pursued by the same group his whole life," Graciela said.

"What do they want with Joshua?" Emmanuel asked.

"First, we need you to help keep an eye on Joshua," Marshall said. "No more camping trips for a while. The group is closing in on our current location. We have to be ready to move him quickly. Understand?"

"Definitely," Emmanuel said. "But why do they want him?"

Marshall and Graciela exchanged glances.

"I thought we could tell you the first part without telling you the whole story, but I guess that's not possible," Marshall said.

"Joshua is a clone of a famous person," Graciela said.

"Cool," Emmanuel responded. "A baseball player? The fans found out?"

"No," Graciela said, "not a baseball player. Remember what we do?"

"Oh, a religious person," Emmanuel said. He thought for a moment. "The Pope?" he asked.

"No," Graciela said, "but you're closer."

"Why are we playing twenty questions?" Marshall asked.

"Joshua was made from material on the Shroud," Graciela said.

"He's a cloth?" Emmanuel asked.

"No, no, genetic material," Graciela said, correcting herself. "DNA."

"Oh my goodness!" he said. His eyes lit up.

Graciela and Marshall nodded to reinforce his insight. There was a knock at the door.

"He doesn't know," Graciela whispered.

"You can't tell him," Marshall whispered.

"He'll be told when he's eighteen," Graciela whispered, as she got up to get the door.

Graciela opened the door.

"Are you ready for lunch?" Joshua asked. "I'm starving."

"Sure," Graciela said.

"You look like you've seen a ghost," Joshua said to Emmanuel.

Emmanuel was unable to speak. His jaw was open and his eyes bulged.

"It looks like your mom should check you out," Joshua said.

At lunch, Emmanuel could not think of anything to say. He just stared at Joshua. Graciela and Marshall asked questions to make small talk. Joshua went back to the buffet three times, and Emmanuel hoped his own behavior would go unnoticed.

Emmanuel had been hungry when he came down the mountain, but now his appetite was gone. Emmanuel's mind was stuck, flipping between thinking about the Jesus he prayed to and the clone of Jesus that he was trying to talk to. In Sunday school, he had been taught that Jesus was his friend, and now the clone of Jesus actually was his friend. Emmanuel's mind raced with thoughts, questions, and connections; but he had to keep them all inside. It was killing him.

"Emmanuel," Joshua said, "you've been looking at me like I'm a freak with two heads or something."

"I'm tired," Emmanuel said. "Maybe I should take a nap."

"You're looking at me the way Maripe looks at me," Joshua said. "I wish I could do something for her."

"I saw how you played with her yesterday," Graciela said. "You do a lot for her."

"No. I wish I could really do something for her, like make her walk," Joshua said.

Graciela and Marshall looked at each other and raised their eyebrows.

"Being a doctor, sometimes I wish I could help people more than I do, too," Graciela said.

"But she just looks at me like she thinks I can do something," Joshua said.

Graciela did not know how to respond. Joshua certainly was sensitive and compassionate. Graciela gently changed the subject by asking more questions about the camping trip.

After lunch, Graciela examined Joshua in their room. Emmanuel told Joshua he was going down to see if Mrs. Parra needed help getting the kids ready for their naps. But actually, Emmanuel wanted to talk to Maripe.

As Graciela listened through her stethoscope, Joshua breathed deeply. "You have some congestion in your lungs," she said. "Right now it's a mild case of walking pneumonia. I don't have any medication for you here. I'll have to get some in town. I want you to lay low for the next few days. No hiking and no swimming."

"I've never been sick in my life," Joshua said.

"Well, you're sick now," Graciela said. "And it could get serious if you don't take care of yourself. Pneumonia is nothing to play around with."

"This will help keep him closer to us so we can protect him," Graciela thought.

When Emmanuel arrived in the day care, all the children were resting on their mats. Maripe was quietly reading a book at a table.

"How was your camping trip?" Maripe asked. "I wish I could go camping."

Emmanuel came straight to the point. "Do you know about Joshua?" he asked.

"Know what?" Maripe asked.

"Who he really is," Emmanuel said.

"Yes," Maripe whispered, "but I can't tell anybody or Mr. Clemente will make me leave right away. I like Jesus— I mean Joshua—even if he never heals me, but I wish he would."

The words touched Emmanuel deeply. He felt a tear forming, but he quickly changed his thoughts, and it stopped.

Emmanuel went out to sit in the lobby so he could have some space to think. *"Joshua wants to heal Maripe,"* Emmanuel thought. *"Maripe wants to be healed, but Joshua doesn't know who he is, so he won't even try. This is crazy. I don't know if Joshua has any healing power, but he should know who he is so he can try. Maripe and all the other sick people who come here deserve that, at least. Somebody is playing around with a lot of people's lives. Joshua should know who he is because everyone should know who they are.*

"Joshua was told that his parents were killed in a car accident. They lied to him. They've moved him around eighteen times. They've lied to him all his life. He needs to know. He's old enough to know. He's twelve years old. He can handle it. By the time he's eighteen, he'll either be kidnapped or he'll be moved another twenty times. It's not right," Emmanuel said to himself. *"I'm his friend and I am going to tell him the truth."*

Just then, Joshua entered the lobby.

"There you are," Joshua said. "I've been looking for you. Maripe said you left the day care."

"Joshua, there's something I have to tell you," Emmanuel said. "I've been acting strange today because I found something out. Maripe is acting weird because she knows, too."

"What?" Joshua asked.

"I don't know if you'll believe me," Emmanuel said. "I know why you've been moved eighteen times."

"You do?" Joshua exclaimed.

"Some people are after you," Emmanuel said.

"What would anybody want with me?" Joshua asked.

Emmanuel hesitated. Then, he blurted it out. "You're a clone of a famous person," he said.

"No way," Joshua said and laughed.

"Really," Emmanuel said. His face was deadly serious.

"A rock star?" Joshua asked. "A soccer star?"

"More famous," Emmanuel answered.

"Stop playing with me," Joshua said. "I don't believe you."

Again, Emmanuel hesitated. "You're the clone of Jesus," he blurted out.

"You're crazy! I won't listen to this nonsense," Joshua cried and started to walk away.

"Give me a minute," Emmanuel demanded, as he grabbed Joshua by the shoulder. "A group of religious fanatics wants to kidnap you, so you can protect them when the world ends. Mr. Clemente lied to you about your parents. They weren't killed in a car accident. You don't have real parents."

"Shut up," Joshua yelled.

"Maripe knows," Emmanuel continued quickly. "She

thinks you can make her walk again. I wouldn't lie to you, Joshua. You're my friend. My parents wouldn't lie to me. I know it's a lot. Think about it. My parents investigate miracles and spiritual mysteries. Why else are they here? We're not on vacation. We're not studying the mountains. We're here because of you. Why are there so many sick people around here?"

"Because the weather is good for their health," Joshua said.

"Because they are doing tests to see if being around you heals them," Emmanuel said.

"Enough," ordered Joshua. "Stop."

"One more thing, and then I'll be quiet," said Emmanuel. "Come here."

Emmanuel led Joshua over to the locked door of Conference Room 101C. He looked through the small slit of a window into the darkened room.

"My parents spend their days in this locked room reading," Emmanuel said. "The table is covered with reports about you. Find a way in there and you'll see I'm right. I am your friend Joshua and I am telling you the truth."

"Leave me alone," Joshua said. "This is a sick joke. You need a doctor worse than I do."

Joshua ran down the hall.

Emmanuel stood in the hallway alone. "*I probably ruined our friendship,*" he thought, as he angrily pounded his fists on the door of Room 101C.

"Even if he doesn't believe me, I had to do it. I have to speak the truth. Oh boy, I'm in trouble. My parents told me not to tell. My parents will be in trouble, too. I hope I did the right thing. I can't live with a lie. But I'm in trouble!"

Sometime after he left Emmanuel, Joshua went to the day care to play checkers with Maripe. He did not believe the crazy story Emmanuel told him. "Why would Emmanuel do it?" Joshua thought. "Why would he say that I have no parents? I have pictures of them. Of all the hurtful things to say, that was really the lowest."

Joshua was very angry with Emmanuel. But still, he had to try one thing. He looked over at Maripe as she stared at the checkerboard studying her next move.

"Maripe," Joshua said.

"Yes," she replied, looking up from the checkerboard.

"Who do people say that I am?" Joshua asked.

Maripe instantly recognized the line from the Bible in Mark 8:27. This was the question Jesus asked his friends. Immediately, she blushed and answered before she could stop herself.

"Jesus the Christ," Maripe said.

Maripe covered her mouth with both hands. She could not take the words back. She had fallen for Joshua's clever use of words.

"Now, he'll send me away," Maripe cried with tears streaming down her face.

"Who's he?" Joshua asked.

"Mr. Clemente," Maripe sobbed.

"It's all right," Joshua said, trying to calm her.

"He said you wouldn't believe me," sniffled Maripe.

"I don't know if I believe you," Joshua said. "But you didn't do anything wrong."

"Now, you won't heal me," cried Maripe.

"If I could heal you I would," Joshua said. "You would be the first one, Maripe. But I don't think I can heal anybody. Least of all, myself."

Joshua coughed several times, then got up from the table and left the room.

Secret Believed

MR. CLEMENTE APPROACHED THE MCCLUES THE NEXT morning while they were at breakfast in the hotel restaurant. Mrs. Ramirez was close behind.

"Have you seen Joshua?" Mr. Clemente asked.

Mrs. Ramirez had a worried look on her face.

"No," Graciela and Marshall answered.

"Me, neither," said Emmanuel.

"No one's seen him," Mr. Clemente said. "His room is empty."

"He never goes anywhere without telling me," said Mrs. Ramirez.

The McClues rose from the table immediately.

"I told him to stay inside because he's sick," Graciela said.

"I'll check the day care and the pool," Emmanuel said.

"We'll search around the first floor," Graciela added, as she and Marshall took off down hallway towards the lobby.

"I'll check the kitchen and the laundry room," Mrs. Ramirez said.

"Everyone meet back at the front desk in five minutes," Mr. Clemente called out.

Emmanuel raced into the day care. Mrs. Parra had just arrived for the day.

"Mrs. Parra, have you seen Joshua this morning?" Emmanuel asked.

She shook her head. Emmanuel darted out of the room, then out to the pool area. Nothing.

They all met back at the front desk in the lobby where Mr. Ramirez was working.

"Let's check his room again for any clues," Graciela said.

Joshua's room was very neatly kept. There were no clothes on the floor. The shelves were dusted.

"Wow," Graciela said to Emmanuel, "look at this clean room."

The bed was neatly made, so they could not tell if it had been slept in.

"Can I see you in the hallway for a moment?" Mr. Clemente asked Graciela and Marshall.

The couple followed him out of the room while Emmanuel and Mrs. Ramirez continued their search.

"I'm calling my people," Mr. Clemente said. "*La Segunda Venida* must have him. I don't know how, but they got him last night or early this morning. We've got to station our men at the airports and at the borders."

"Are you sure? We haven't checked outside yet," Marshall said.

"Every minute we wait is another minute they can get him out of the country. Blast! I knew they were close but we've always spotted them before," Mr. Clemente said and ran down the hall.

Emmanuel continued poking around Joshua's room. *"Joshua hasn't been kidnapped. He finally believed me and he's run away,"* Emmanuel thought. *"But I'm not going to say a word to anyone until I'm sure."*

Marshall came back into the room.

"Emmanuel, get Speagle and we'll go outside and look around."

Relieved that his dad did not suspect anything, Emmanuel raced out of the room and up the three flights of stairs to get Speagle out of her cage.

Marshall, Emmanuel, and a leashed Speagle trooped around the grounds behind the hotel. Emmanuel kept eyeing the ski run, and looking toward the mountaintop. Speagle acted as if she were out for a regular walk. They checked around the maintenance building and the building that housed the motor for the ski lift. They found nothing.

"What would have made Joshua believe me?" Emmanuel thought. *"What changed his mind?"* He had a sudden insight. *"Oh my goodness!"* he thought.

"Dad," he said Emmanuel urgently, "let's go back inside to see if they know anything."

Marshall nodded that he was ready to give up. Emmanuel raced away with Speagle back into the hotel. They made a straight line toward the day care. By the time they arrived Mr. Clemente was already there. He was talk-ing to Maripe in the corner of the room. He sat in a short chair so he was at eye level with Maripe in her wheelchair. Mrs. Parra met Emmanuel at the entrance to the room as she was waiting for the other children to arrive.

"Maripe was upset when she arrived," Mrs. Parra said to Emmanuel. "Then when she found out Joshua was miss-ing, she just started sobbing uncontrollably. Luckily, Mr. Clemente came by to calm her down."

"*That's not why Mr. Clemente came by,*" Emmanuel thought. Emmanuel walked briskly across the room.

"It's all my fault!" Maripe sobbed.

"You told didn't you?" Mr. Clemente said sternly.

"He tricked me!" cried Maripe. "It just came out before I knew it!"

"You know what will happen to you because you told," Mr. Clemente said.

"It was an accident," Maripe said. "Please don't send me away."

Emmanuel arrived right behind Mr. Clemente.

"I told Joshua," exclaimed Emmanuel. "Leave Maripe alone. Joshua didn't believe me at first, so he tricked her into telling him."

Mr. Clemente wheeled around in his chair to face Emmanuel.

"You!" screamed Mr. Clemente.

Speagle barked sharply at him.

"And how did you know!?" Mr. Clemente screamed, causing Speagle to bark even more loudly.

"We told him," Graciela interjected, as she and Marshall arrived on the scene.

"This is just great!" Mr. Clemente ranted. "Can't anybody in your family keep a secret!?"

"Don't talk to my son like that!" Graciela yelled back.

"Wait until I tell your benefactor," Mr. Clemente said. "Everything was going according to plan until you McClues arrived. Why did you tell him, young man?"

"Because you've lied to Joshua all his life," Emmanuel said. "He thinks his parents died in a car accident. He believes he's been moved around because no one loves him. He doesn't think anyone could love him."

"He has everything he needs," Mr. Clemente said. "I've given my whole life to him."

"You haven't given him what he really needs," responded Emmanuel. "You haven't given him love and a family."

"So, where is he now?" Mr. Clemente asked, ignoring Emmanuel.

"I think he ran away to the mountain," Emmanuel answered. "I bet his camping gear is gone."

Mr. Clemente ran to the storage room with the McClues and Speagle in close pursuit.

Joshua's camping equipment was not there.

"Now, I've got to get a search team," Mr. Clemente huffed. "Do you know where he is?"

"No," Emmanuel said. "You won't find him. He knows that mountain better than anyone."

"We'll see about that," Mr. Clemente replied, as he stormed off, leaving them in the storage room.

"I'm sorry, Mom and Dad," Emmanuel said. "I was going to tell you. I just had to tell Joshua the truth."

"I wish you would have talked it over with us first," Graciela said.

"I know," Emmanuel said.

"But I think you did the right thing," Graciela said.

"So do I," said Marshall.

"You do?" Emmanuel asked with surprise.

Graciela nodded. "Joshua has been lied to and treated like a lab rat long enough. The truth is always the best thing even though it's not the most popular."

"Are you in trouble again?" Emmanuel asked.

"No more than usual," Graciela said.

"Is Ben going to fire you?" Emmanuel asked.

"I have no idea," his mother answered. "We do have to find Joshua, though. I'm worried about his health. Hiking is going to make his pneumonia much worse."

"He's going to be tough to find," Emmanuel said. "Look, he took the little stove. He won't even be starting a campfire tonight."

Graciela hugged her son.

"Emmanuel, you did a very tough and very brave thing," she said.

Within an hour, a helicopter flew over the hotel. The McClues ran outside to get a closer look. It flew low over the trees and up the side of the mountain. When it reached the top, it flew in ever-widening circles. After several minutes, it flew back down the mountain over a different part of the forest. It was gradually searching the whole mountain area.

An hour later a large truck arrived. Twenty men in police-like uniforms filed out of the back of the truck. Two of the men had large German shepherds on leashes. As soon as he saw the large dogs, Emmanuel picked up Speagle.

The men spread out around the base of the mountain and began the long trek up. They kept each other in view so they could cover every part. The McClues stayed outside all day to watch the search operations.

"Mr. Clemente's plan is falling apart before his eyes," Graciela said. "I don't think he ever imagined that Joshua would run away."

"It was just too much for Joshua," Emmanuel said. "What would you do if you found out that you were a clone of Jesus?"

"I don't think Mr. Clemente thought that Joshua would believe it if anybody told him," Marshall said.

"He didn't believe me at first," Emmanuel said, "but when Maripe said it, too, he knew that the both of us are more trustworthy than Mr. Clemente."

"If you had told us that you were going to tell Joshua, we could have figured out how to take care of him after he found out," Marshall said.

"I am very, very sorry," Emmanuel said.

"It's all right. I admire your courage for speaking the truth," Marshall said.

"The important thing now is that we find Joshua and bring him back safely," Graciela said.

The helicopter flew away back to its base to refuel. The men on foot hiked back down the mountain during the late afternoon. They had not spotted a thing. The helicopter returned about the time the men reached the base of the mountain. As dusk was turning to dark, the helicopter made several trips up and down the mountain again. It was trying to spot a campfire. Eventually, it gave up.

A storm moved in over the mountain. This one was not going to blow over quickly like the one that caught Emmanuel and Joshua on their camping trip. This one was going to linger over the mountain and give steady rain all night long.

The McClues went inside to get out of the weather. They took Emmanuel into Conference Room 101C.

"As long as you know everything you might as well come in," Marshall said.

"We can watch the mountain from the windows in here," Graciela said.

It had been a long day. They were all tired and very sad. Emmanuel looked at the piles of reports strewn around the big table.

"*What a strange thing to have your life recorded in so much detail*," Emmanuel thought, as he flipped through the reports toward the bottom of a pile. A title caught his eye: "Loss of Life in the Joshua Project."

"What's this one about?" Joshua asked, handing it to his mom.

"Cloning is a terrible thing, Emmanuel," she said. "Most clones die before they are born. Mr. Clemente knew this so he tried to make multiple clones of Jesus so, at least, one would live. According to the report, Joshua was the only one that was born a healthy baby. The rest died. Some were miscarriages. Others were stillborn. Still others lived a few days before their birth defects took their lives. Many babies died while Mr. Clemente was trying to make a clone of Jesus."

Emmanuel shook his head. "That's awful," he said.

Another title caught Emmanuel's eye: "Health Problems in Adult Clones."

"Have you read this one?" Emmanuel asked, as he showed it to his mom.

"No," said Graciela, "Why?"

"Joshua said he's never been sick before," Emmanuel said. "Suddenly, on our camping trip he started coughing, and he couldn't walk very far without resting."

"You're right," Graciela said. "I've heard that cloned animals which are healthy when they are young suddenly develop many health problems when they become adults. Problems often occur with the lungs, heart, and the immune system. They can't fight off disease very well."

"Why's that?" Emmanuel asked.

"Scientists think there are random errors in the cloning process that don't show up until adulthood," Graciela said. "Healthy animals suddenly develop bad health and die young."

"Joshua is twelve," Emmanuel said.

"Oh my goodness," Graciela gasped, as she pieced it together. "We've got to find Joshua quickly. It's not only that he's got pneumonia. His immune system is probably weakened, and he can't recover like a normal person."

"Emmanuel, do you have any idea where Joshua might hide?" Marshall asked.

"Joshua has lots of trails marked on the mountain," Emmanuel said. "We were on the trail marked with stars. He carved a small star in a tree about every fifty meters."

"What were the other trails?" Marshal asked.

"There are trails marked with crosses, squares, circles, and triangles, I think."

"If you were Joshua where would you go if you really wanted to hide?" Marshall asked.

"Well, he took his stove so he didn't need a campfire," said Emmanuel. "It must have worked because the helicopter didn't find a fire or even a tent. I've got it! The cave!"

Emmanuel eyes lit up. "One of the trails leads to a cave," exclaimed Emmanuel. "If I were Joshua that's where I would go."

"Good, Emmanuel," Marshall said. "Which trail leads to the cave?"

"It can't be the star trail because we used that one," Emmanuel said. "I remember! The circle trail!"

"Good work, Emmanuel. It makes sense that Joshua would hide in the cave," Marshall said.

"Hopefully, Mr. Clemente's crew will search all the trails at the same time tomorrow," Graciela said.

"I don't know if Mr. Clemente will listen to us after the

trouble we've caused him," Marshall said. "If he doesn't, we'll hike up tomorrow on the circle trail to find Joshua. Right, Emmanuel?"

"Right," Emmanuel said.

Just then, a line of six identical black SUVs pulled into the hotel driveway under the cover of darkness. Their darkly tinted windows blended in with the dark of the night. Four men got out of each vehicle. All were wearing identical dark blue suits. Some ran around the hotel to the left while others circled the hotel to the right. The remaining men surrounded the fifth SUV where a gray-haired man with a narrow face and a thin mustache emerged. They circled around their gray-haired leader and briskly walked into the hotel.

The McClues heard noises coming down the hall from near the front desk. Marshall went out to check but only got a step outside before he backed his way into the conference room. A moment later Mr. Clemente, in his usual light blue suit, was pushed into the room by two of the dark-suited men. Following them was the gray-haired leader and two more dark-suited men. At least three more stood out in the hallway.

Graciela rushed over to pull Emmanuel close to her. She did a double-take. The gray-haired leader in the dark blue suit was a thin version of Mr. Clemente. On his narrow face was a thin mustache. His steely, dark eyes sized up the situation.

"Yes, Mrs. McClue," the gray-haired leader said. "Mr. Clemente and I are brothers. I haven't seen my dear brother Miguel in a little over fifteen years. It has taken this long to finally catch up to him."

"He's not here, Horatio," Mr. Clemente said. "He ran away last night. He found out."

"What convenient timing," Horatio sneered. "My men are searching the place as we speak. We have a little time before they report in, so I'll tell you a little story. You see, Mrs. McClue, my brother used to be part of *La Segunda Venida*, but he stole from us the DNA from the Shroud and formed his own little group."

"Then you're the ones who broke into the Cathedral in Turin fifteen years ago," Graciela exclaimed.

"You were scared to do the cloning, Horatio," Mr. Clemente said, ignoring Graciela's comment. "You had everything you needed, but you were afraid to make Joshua and begin the end of the world. But I wasn't afraid."

"We were waiting for the right time, but you became impatient," Horatio said. "Now we need Joshua so he can protect us from the end of the world."

Another dark-suited man came into the room and shook his head at Horatio.

"I am tired of waiting for the boy, Miguel," said Horatio. "Until you turn him over, I'll take another boy in his place."

"NO!" Graciela screamed, as she tightened her grip on Emmanuel. "You're not taking Emmanuel!"

Three dark-suited men moved toward Emmanuel as Marshall stepped in their way.

"Don't make us use force," Horatio said. He reached inside his suit jacket threatening to pull out a gun.

The other dark-suited men reached inside their suit jackets, too. No guns were seen, but the message was clear.

"When you give us Joshua, you'll get Emmanuel back," Horatio said.

Marshall let the men go around him, but they had to pry Emmanuel loose from Graciela. The men led a twisting and squirming Emmanuel across the room toward the door. Horatio looked at his brother and scowled.

"Think he's safe? Think again!" Horatio snarled.

Those words! Those same words that Graciela first heard from the demon in London, then in her dream, now were spoken as her son was being kidnapped. The demon's threat had come true, acted out by men in dark blue suits. It was too much. She fainted into her husband's arms.

Secret Redeemed

EMMANUEL WAS HANDCUFFED AND BLINDFOLDED AND driven for what seemed like two hours. Finally, he was dragged from the car and put in a room with no windows. As soon as the handcuffs were removed, he ripped off the blindfold. He got a glimpse of his room, which amounted to a metal bed and a toilet, before the door slammed shut leaving him in total darkness. He was not afraid—exactly. He was more shocked and numb. He had imagined situations like this many times during spy movies. He felt his way around the room, bumping into the toilet and the bed before he climbed onto the bed. In all the spy movies he saw, the spies always had a special device in their shoe that helped them out of their jam. Emmanuel had nothing in his shoe and nothing up his sleeve.

As he lay in the dark, reality began to set in. "*I could be here a long time,*" he thought. "*They might even try to get me*

*to tell them where Joshua is . . . What will I say? . . . I wonder
how Dad is doing. I know how Mom is doing. She is freaking out.
Poor Dad! He has to be there with Mom."*

Emmanuel woke up many times during the night. Each time he awoke he forgot where he was before he was suddenly snapped back to reality. This was not a dream. It was real. During the night, Emmanuel realized something important. Any group that claimed to be religious would not use guns, kidnapping, and force. *La Segunda Venida* claimed to be religious, but really they had no idea what Jesus and religion were all about.

In the morning a little bit of light came under the door. The door swung open for a moment and a tray slid into the room. The door slammed again. The buzz of a fluorescent light started above him. In the new light, Emmanuel's eyes adjusted, and he went over to the tray. Oatmeal and orange juice.

Graciela paced most of the night. This was a parent's worst nightmare. She was supposed to protect Emmanuel, but now she was powerless to do her duty. If anything happened to him, it would be more painful than if it happened to her directly. She prayed but nothing brought her comfort. She kept thinking of Emmanuel being hurt, scared, maybe even beaten. And that in order to get Emmanuel back she would have to trade Joshua for him. She could not do that, either.

"Oh God, protect both boys!" she prayed. She continued to pray, but it did not seem to help her.

Marshall did not sleep well, but he did sleep a couple hours. Graciela woke him at first light and the two got ready to hike up the mountain to find Joshua. They could not do anything to help Emmanuel right now, but they had to do something. Inaction would have driven them crazy. So they focused their energy on trying to help Joshua. They were going to find the circle trail that led to the cave.

They went to tell Mr. Clemente of their plan. Maybe he would give them men to help them search.

"I don't want anything to do with you," Mr. Clemente said before they could utter a word.

"We really don't want anything to do with you either," Graciela said.

"But we have to work together," Marshall said.

"No, we don't," Mr. Clemente replied. "You ruined everything."

"Your brother caught you completely by surprise," Graciela said. "If Joshua hadn't run away, they would have taken him. Instead, they have Emmanuel."

That statement got Mr. Clemente's attention.

"Emmanuel gave us some information about a trail and a cave," Marshall said. "We're going up that trail to the cave. We could use some of your men to help."

"My men will comb the entire mountain and not just one little trail," Mr. Clemente scoffed.

"You didn't find anything yesterday," Graciela said.

"Today will be different," barked Mr. Clemente.

Graciela and Marshall left to find Mr. and Mrs. Ramirez.

"We'll take a walkie-talkie," Marshall told Mr. Ramirez. "We'll radio you if we find anything."

"I know Joshua is all right," Mrs. Ramirez said behind a worried smile. "He is a great camper."

They did not take any camping gear, just water bottles, a medical bag, food, a walkie-talkie, flashlights, and binoculars. They got Speagle and off they went. The grass was wet from the rain the night before. The forest floor was soggy and, at times, muddy. In this weather, Joshua was probably so sick he could not hike back down even if he wanted to.

The first trick was to find a tree marked with a circle. They walked along the edge of the forest for about a hundred meters and found no marks on any of the trees. They went a few trees into the forest and checked as they walked backed toward where they started. They found a tree with a small triangle scratched into it about a meter off the ground. Still no circle. They walked farther back. There was one with a square. Walking a bit farther, they found a circle!

"Finding the first tree is going to be the tough part," they thought. It took forty-minutes to find it. It takes two points to make a straight line, and standing at the first circled tree, they had to decide which direction to walk to look for the second point. Graciela stayed at the circle-marked tree with Speagle while Marshall headed out in a direction straight up the mountain. According to

Emmanuel, the next mark would be about fifty meters up. Marshall counted out fifty strides then began searching the area for a tree with a mark. He found nothing.

"Either I went in the wrong direction, or I didn't walk far enough," Marshall shouted to Graciela.

"This is more difficult than I thought," she shouted back.

Joshua did not travel these trails very often so there was no worn path on the ground. The rain had washed away any footprints that might have been there. Marshall continued searching in an arc about fifty meters from the first tree. No luck. He walked up the mountain about ten more strides and repeated the search in an arc about sixty meters from the first tree. Still nothing. Ten more strides up the mountain and he repeated the search. There it was, the second circle-marked tree! It took them an hour to find the second tree.

"At this rate, we'll never get there," Marshall yelled.

"I've got an idea," Graciela said.

Graciela took out the binoculars and focused them so she got a close-up of the circle-mark next to where Marshall was standing. It came in very clearly. She then walked uphill, stood next to Marshall, and looked through the binoculars making sure she did not change the focus. Trees at about seventy meters distance became clear in the viewfinder. She searched the area ahead of her and sure enough she spotted the next circle-marked tree.

"Fantastic!" Marshall said.

Graciela's new method did not always work. Sometimes they had to search on foot for a few minutes before they found the next tree, but things went much more quickly.

Joshua's trail was not a straight line. It was a gently curving trail that took them to the right side of the mountain. As they moved up the mountain, they tried not to think about Emmanuel. They concentrated on what they could control, searching for Joshua, and this kept their spirits up. About mid-morning they heard the helicopter go overhead. Once it paused curiously above them before moving on. They ignored it.

They neared the top about noon. They came to an area where they could not climb any higher. A wall of rock jutted out of the ground in front of them. They had to go right or left and wind their way up to the top. Graciela looked both ways with her binoculars but there were very few trees around to be markers. Marshall walked around inspecting the trees, for he thought the next marker would be much closer than seventy meters. They had come to a fork in the road and had to decide very carefully whether to go right or left. Graciela moved along next to the rock while Speagle tagged along on her leash. Suddenly, Speagle sniffed the air then disappeared behind some brush covering the rock. Graciela continued walking along until the leash became tight, then turned around to see that Speagle was gone. Graciela followed the leash to where it disappeared, then moved back the brush with her hand to reveal a large opening in the rock. The leash was being dragged deeper into the dark opening as Speagle went farther and farther.

"Over here!" Graciela called to Marshall.

Graciela got down on her knees, pulled out her flashlight, and crawled in. Suddenly, the leash became still. A piercing sound rang out through the cave. Graciela jumped back. It was Speagle's bark. With her flashlight beam, she saw an amazing sight! Speagle was wagging her tail and licking the face of Joshua who lay very still wrapped up in his sleeping bag. He was still alive, but in bad shape. His lungs rattled and wheezed. He tried to speak but could only cough with a pained look on his face.

Graciela backed out of the cave so Marshall could go in and lift Joshua out. Marshall could not stand in the cave so he stooped low to the ground and carried Joshua out.

"Good girl," Graciela said to Speagle as the dog licked her face.

Marshall set Joshua down outside then got on the walkie-talkie. Graciela gave Joshua a drink of water. He was dehydrated, as well.

"Mr. Ramirez," Marshall said, "we found Joshua."

There was a yell of excitement on the other end mixed with a lot of static. Speagle barked.

"Thank you," Mr. Ramirez exclaimed. "Thank you both so much."

"Joshua is too weak to walk," Marshall said. "Can you signal the helicopter?"

"The helicopter can't land on the mountain," responded Mr. Ramirez. "You have to get to a clear area. Can you see the ski run from where you are?"

Marshall looked over. From their high vantage point they could see part of the ski run and several towers of the ski lift.

"Yes," Marshall said.

"Can you carry Joshua there?" Mr. Ramirez asked.

"It's probably about two kilometers," Marshall said. "Yes, we can get him there."

"You can take him down the ski lift," Mr. Ramirez said. "I'll turn it on."

"Great," Marshall said. "We'll see you there."

"Can't wait to see you!" Mr. Ramirez said.

Marshall picked up Joshua. He was about as heavy as Emmanuel and Marshall had stopped trying to carry Emmanuel years ago. Graciela walked in front of him to guide his steps. They would not have to climb down very much. They were headed down a gentle angle over to the start of the ski run. Joshua looked like he was in a cocoon all sealed up in his sleeping bag. Graciela kept giving Joshua and Marshall small sips of water. Marshall's arms began to ache, but he kept them locked in place as he moved forward step by step. With constant encouragement from Graciela, Marshall made steady progress. He was afraid that if he set Joshua down, he would not be able to pick him up again, so he kept moving forward with no rest. Graciela kept talking to Joshua, too, encouraging him to hang in there and take it easy.

They could hear the whirring motor of the ski lift now and the click-clack of the seat supports going over the pulleys. The last two hundred meters were endless. Marshall went into a zone of concentration, like he used to when he ran cross-country in high school. He ignored all pain and focused on keeping each foot moving forward. Finally, they emerged from the trees into the clearing of the ski run. The ski lift was straight ahead of them. Mustering his last bit of strength, Marshall gently set Joshua down on a moving seat. Graciela sat next to Joshua and rested his head in her lap. Marshall grabbed Speagle and hopped onto the next moving seat.

The helicopter flew over. The search team came out of the forest with their German shepherds in tow. Speagle barked at them from way up in his sky chair. Riding the ski lift down was like being a hero riding in a parade. The hotel loomed before them. An ambulance's emergency lights flashed below.

Graciela rode in the ambulance. An oxygen mask was put on Joshua and Graciela started an I.V. for dehydration. She gave him a shot of antibiotics. Mr. and Mrs. Ramirez followed the ambulance in their car. Marshall and Speagle rode in the back seat.

Once at the hospital, Marshall had to wait outside with Speagle. After Joshua was checked over in the emergency room, he was admitted and assigned his own room on the third floor. Mr. and Mrs. Ramirez and Graciela stood in Joshua's room while the nurses made him comfortable, adjusting both his I.V. and the level of oxygen coming to his mask.

Not long after Joshua got settled in, Mr. Clemente came into his room followed by his brother Horatio and two dark-suited men.

"You're not taking Joshua anywhere!" Graciela said, pointing her finger at Horatio. "You have a lot of nerve coming here!"

Horatio ignored her and walked around the bed slowly inspecting Joshua.

"We're not trading Joshua for Emmanuel, either," Graciela said. "We love our son, but we're not giving up Joshua to get Emmanuel back."

"To protect us at the end of the world we need someone who can brave great storms of fire, massive earthquakes, and earth-shattering explosions," Horatio said in an arrogant tone. "We can't rely on someone who is so weak that he gets pneumonia merely from camping."

"That is not how God works," Graciela said.

"That is your opinion," Horatio snapped back, pointing a finger in her face. "The Second Coming of Jesus brings on the end of the world. Cloning Jesus is the Second Coming. Those with Jesus will be protected. We are creating our own protector."

"You're deranged," Graciela said.

Horatio ignored her and turned back to Joshua.

"This sickly boy cannot possibly be Jesus," said Horatio. "Jesus is perfect in every way. Jesus would never get sick."

"Jesus was like us in all things but sin, so why couldn't he get sick like we do," Graciela thought.

"Fortunately for us, there is another...," Horatio stopped himself in mid-sentence.

"Another what?" asked Graciela.

"Another option," said Horatio, choosing his words carefully. He picked up his cell phone and dialed.

"Return the boy," Horatio said.

"What option?" Graciela persisted.

Horatio and his two dark-suited sidekicks headed for the door.

"You can keep your sickly boy, my dear brother," Horatio sneered, "and you can have your son back, Mrs. McClue. I am on to greater things."

With that, Horatio and his men were gone.

A dazed Graciela did not pause for long before she went on the attack with Mr. Clemente.

"As for you," Graciela said with a finger in Mr. Clemente's face, "Your sick experiment is over. Joshua is going to have his own life now."

Joshua signaled to Graciela that he wanted to say something. He could not speak, so she gave him a pen and pad of paper. As he wrote, Graciela read it out loud.

"No more lies, Mr. Clemente," wrote Joshua. "I want to live in truth. I don't have real parents because I am a clone, but I would like Mr. and Mrs. Ramirez to be my parents, if they will have me."

"Oh, yes," Mrs. Ramirez said.

"Absolutely," Mr. Ramirez said.

Mr. and Mrs. Ramirez hugged each other then each held Joshua's hand.

"We love you just for who you are, Joshua," Mr. Ramirez said.

"It would give us great joy to be your parents," Mrs. Ramirez said.

Mr. Clemente left the room in a huff. Graciela followed him into the hallway.

"Wait a minute!" she demanded.

But Mr. Clemente kept walking.

"How do you know our benefactor?" Graciela called out.

"We go back a long way," said Mr. Clemente said over his shoulder. "I thought we were friends, until you were sent here."

Mr. Clemente disappeared into the stairwell. Graciela went back into Joshua's room. She saw that Joshua had written some more, so she read it aloud.

"I am not Jesus," wrote Joshua. "I am more like Lazarus. I was all wrapped up in my cave. It would have become my tomb. Thank you, Mrs. McClue, for saving my life."

"You are very welcome," said Graciela, as the tears welled up in her eyes.

Mr. and Mrs. Ramirez stayed at the hospital while Graciela, Marshall, and Speagle drove back to the hotel in the Ramirez's car. By the time they reached the hotel, Emmanuel was waving and jumping up and down outside the front door. The car stopped. Marshall reached Emmanuel first and lifted him into the air. His arms ached from carrying Joshua, but that did not stop him from celebrating his son's return. Graciela moved in. She hugged her son and cried on his shoulder. Speagle barked and jumped up at their knees.

"Are you hurt?" asked Graciela.

"No," Emmanuel said. "They locked me in a room, but they fed me. They gave me oatmeal and orange juice for breakfast."

His parents laughed in relief.

The McClues sat in the dark on pool chairs a little ways away from the side of the hotel. Speagle rested in Emmanuel's lap. They wanted to get away from the hotel lights so they could enjoy looking up at the stars. It seemed right to look up and take in the big picture of the universe above them.

"I am afraid we haven't seen the last of the Clemente brothers," Graciela said.

"Let's forget about them for a while," responded Emmanuel. "Will Joshua get better?"

"I think he'll recover this time," Graciela said. "Joshua wanted me to tell him everything, the whole truth, so I told him that his health might be weakening because adult clones tend to develop many health problems from errors in the cloning process. I told him that he will have to be examined by specialists that know more about the cloning process."

"What did he say to all that?" asked Marshall.

"He said he wants to live the best life he can with Mr. and Mrs. Ramirez, even if he doesn't have a whole lot of time left," Graciela said.

"He is a remarkable young man," said Marshall.

"Joshua isn't remarkable because he's the clone of Jesus," Graciela said. "He's remarkable because of who he is all by himself."

"I know," Marshall said.

"I think I know what might be the worst thing about cloning," pondered Graciela.

"What's that?" asked Marshall.

"A clone has to live their whole life being compared to someone else who has already lived," she said.

"It's hard enough growing up trying to discover who you are. Can you imagine trying to do that while constantly being compared to someone else who lived before you? God sees the uniqueness of each person, but cloning makes it much harder for us humans to see the uniqueness of each person."

Just then a car with bright headlights pulled into the hotel driveway.

"Who's that?" asked Marshall.

A woman got out of the car. The driver started unloading her many suitcases and garment bags.

"Speaking of being unique," Graciela said.

"Jordana!" Emmanuel exclaimed, as he and Speagle raced over to her.

"What an adventure!" Jordana declared, as she gave Emmanuel a big hug.

"This must be Speagle. What a cute little doggie. I don't know what your mission has been, but it could not have been half as exciting as my adventure. I searched the world for you, Emmanuel. First, Boston. No Emmanuel. Then, Italy. Still, no Emmanuel. And then, on the way to Argentina . . . "

Graciela and Marshall just looked at each other and smiled.